16 WISHES

The Novelization

Based on the screenplay by Annie DeYoung

MARVISTA
entertainment
www.16WishesTheMovie.com

inkmedia™

Ink Media Corporation
120 Kisco Avenue Suite D
Mount Kisco NY 10549
Visit our website at www.inkmedia.com
Email us at info@inkmedia.com

First edition: June 2010

Printed in the United States of America (LPTN)
Printed by SBI
Chelsea, Mi
6-15-2010
317566
ISBN: 978-1-60515-563-0

I need *privacy* and *boundaries*. I need my own *space*. I have been looking forward to this day all my life and now that it's here, I *wish* you would all *get out* and stop spoiling it!"

Abby succeeds in herding them all into the hallway. Then she slams the door hard - right in their faces. Her parents and brother stand outside the door, a bit stunned. The wind from the slamming door has blown out all the candles on the cake. Suddenly, Abby yanks the door open again. "Love you!" she adds, and then slams the door shut once more.

Abby turns away from the door, and catches a glimpse of herself in the mirror on the armoire. Time to remove the pore-cleaning strip. In one swift movement, she pulls it off. "Ow, ow, ow!" she cries. Then, looking down at the strip, she adds, "Ew," before throwing the nasty thing away. She looks back in the mirror. Much better. She smiles. "I'm sixteen," she says to her reflection. "This day is going to be *magical*."

Abby is so caught up in her plans for the day that she doesn't even notice the cool, vintage van that has just squealed to a stop in front of her house. On the side of the van are the words Bugs-B-Gone. The van sits idling for a moment before a cute, perky young woman hops out. She is slim, brisk and very professional in her movements and she wears a jumpsuit with a name patch— Celeste— over the pocket. But apart from her general air of professionalism, there is something different about her. Maybe it's the extra twinkly look in her eyes, or the bounce in her step; it's almost as if her feet don't quite touch the ground when she walks. As she strides up to the front door of the Jensen's house, a large wasp buzzes around her face. Far from concerned, she seems to communicate with the wasp. With a wink from Celeste, it goes flying toward Abby's house.

The wasp buzzes off, and flies into a tiny air conditioning vent in the attic, where there is a huge wasps' nest. The wasp hovers in front of the nest, buzzing. The nest seems to buzz back, with a low-pitched, menacing, million-wasp rumble. Celeste takes out a flyer from the folder she's carrying and tucks it near the doorknob; as she does, the flyer gives off a magical little shimmer.

In the kitchen, Abby's mom is preparing breakfast while Mike sits at the table, "playing" a digital toy guitar. Abby's mom puts the birthday cake down in front of him. When she turns to walk back to the stove, he swipes a finger through the frosting. Abby's dad walks into the room.

"I told you guys she wouldn't like our little surprise," Mike says when he sees his father.

"I don't understand her," says Abby's dad.

"She's probably just nervous about her Sweet Sixteen party tonight," her mom says. "Oh Bob, the party lights! They're in the garage."

"I'm on it," he says and goes off in search of the lights.

Abby's mom hands Mike a plate piled high with eggs, bacon and a freshly baked blueberry muffin.

"Wow, thanks!" says Mike, picking up his fork.

"Uh uh, that's for your sister," she says. She grabs the fork before he can dig in.

Meanwhile, Abby is upstairs, tossing outfits onto her bed like confetti. "Too yellow," she says to one discarded outfit. "Too blue, too pink." She is so intent on her task that she doesn't notice the wasp buzzing softly behind the vent. It hangs suspended, as if it is watching her. "Too nighttime, too daytime, too *fifteen*..."

Finally, she selects a blue and violet ensemble and lays it out on her bed. "Perfect," she breathes, just as Mike bursts into the room, the toy guitar on his back.

"Hey Abs," he begins.

"Hello!" says Abby, annoyed. "Knock much?"

Mike steps back and raps on the open door in a half-hearted way.

"What?" asks Abby.

"Mom made you a special birthday breakfast."

"Aw, that's sweet. Just put it there," says Abby.

Mike slings the guitar into his lap, settles into Abby's desk chair and helps himself to a slice of bacon from the heaping plate.

"Not you. The food."

"Two secs," Mike says, mouth stuffed with bacon. He strums the toy guitar and begins to sing. "They say it's your breakfast." He jumps up and twists like a rock star. "But I'm gonna eat it, da-da-da-dum, da-da-dum."

Abby watches this little performance thinking, *what a dork.*

"You do know that's not a real guitar," she finally says.

Mike spins around, ready to execute a serious, rock star power-strum. He sends his arm flying out, and when he does, he knocks Abby's jewelry box off her desk. It goes crashing to the floor and the contents, including a thick wad of cash, spill out all over.

"Mike!" says Abby. She quickly kneels down to gather everything up. The cash is the very first thing she stuffs back into the box.

"Wow," says Mike as he watches her. "Can I have a loan?" Before she can answer, he starts circling around her room, as if checking out what else of value she might be hiding.

"No," says Abby firmly. "You can *not* have a loan. I've been saving for my party tonight." Her voice softens and grows all misty around the edges. *"The best Sweet Sixteen party ever."*

"Ah yes," Mike says dryly. "Wish number fifteen."

"What?" says Abby. Then she sees that Mike is looking at the list.

Mike starts reading aloud from the list. *"When I'm sixteen, I'll have the best Sweet Sixteen party ever."*

"Hey!" she says. "That list is private."

"Not. You honestly thought you'd get all this today?"

"I'm an essentially hopeful person," says Abby, slightly embarrassed.

"The first one's hilarious. *When I'm sixteen, I'll meet Joey Lockhart.*" Mike smirks. "*The* Joey Lockhart?" Abby looks over at the poster of Joey in his way-cool hat and quickly steps in front of it to shield it from her brother's view. "He's an international pop star with about a bazillion fans. Why would you even wish that?" Mike asks.

"I was seven," Abby says.

"You were delusional," retorts Mike.

"You were five and wore a cape...to *school.*" Abby narrows her eyes for emphasis. "Anyway, my other wishes are more realistic." Mike looks unconvinced, so Abby continues. "Like Wish Number Three: When I'm sixteen, I'll decorate my room the way I want."

Abby closes her eyes and remembers the dream she had when she made that wish: she's seven years old, sitting in a director's chair with her name stenciled on the back and giving directions through an old fashioned megaphone. A line of adult decorators and contractors are waiting their turn to show her various decorating options, including fabric and carpet samples, paint chips and wallpaper samples. In her fantasy, seven year old Abby jumps from the chair and walks down the line, selecting the most adorable fabric, the softest carpet and the prettiest wallpaper pattern.

Mike breaks in, interrupting her reverie. "Mmm, Abs? Wish number three? Not a good idea."

"Why not?" she asks.

"If you decorate the way you dress..." He stops to cringe. "Ouch!" Abby punches him lightly. "Ooh, that tickles." He turns back to the list. "So what's with the mug shot on sixteen?"

"It's not a mug shot," says Abby defensively. "It's Logan Buchanan."

"You have a crush on the quarterback? How cliché," says Mike.

"For your information, he's also in the Drama Club and once attended Chess Masters."

"I know. I was *there*," drawls Mike. "He wanted to buy my chem notes!"

"Well, I think he's perfect," says Abby, raising her chin a little and looking her brother straight in the eye. "And if I get my wish, he'll talk to me today."

In the street below, a car horn blares. Abby goes to the window. Mike joins her in looking out. There, parked in the driveway across the street, is a shiny new yellow car. Written on the back window are the words, HAPPY BIRTHDAY KITTEN!

Abby scowls as she sees Krista Cook, her arch rival, holding up the car keys and squealing with delight. Krista is pretty, albeit in an uptight sort of way. She blows a kiss to her parents, who are standing proudly in the driveway in front of the car. Then Krista looks across the street, right up into Abby's window. Abby knows she can see her. And she knows that when

Krista lifts the glittering keys in her direction, their merry jingling sound is directed right at her. Krista, Abby realizes, is gloating. It makes Abby's blood boil.

"Cool car," breathes Mike.

"It's not cool," says Abby, pouting. "It's terrible. I don't know what I did to deserve this. Why was Krista, of all people, born on the same day I was?"

"Yeah," says Mike. "It must be so annoying, the way she always gets better stuff for her birthday."

"I have no idea why she hates me so much," says Abby, continuing to glare at Krista. "Ever since third grade, she's tried to ruin my birthday."

"Which is also her birthday," Mike points out.

Abby turns to her brother. *"Why* are you still here? Get out!" She hustles him out of the room, and into the hall. Then she slams the door. "Dibs on the bathroom!" she calls out quickly. After a moment, she emerges, still wearing her pink jammies and her bunny slippers. and heads for the bathroom. Time to do her hair and her makeup. Everything has to be perfect because today she's going to create the look of the newly minted sixteen-year-old girl that she is.

Half an hour later, every cream, lotion and makeup product in the bathroom cabinet is spread out on the counter. The place is a disaster, but Abby looks lovely.

Mike approaches the bathroom door and tries the knob. It's

locked. He sighs, exasperated. "C'mon, Abs!" he calls out in frustration. "You've been in there for a year."

"Thirty two minutes," replies Abby. "Most girls take twice that long." Mike continues to pound on the door. "Hold your horses!" Abby says. She applies a final coat of lip gloss and surveys the effect in the mirror. Perfect. Outside the bathroom, Mike continues his pounding, which reverberates all the way up into the attic.

The lone wasp that was circling around earlier zips up to the nest, quivering with an excited, high-pitched buzz. The wasps in the nest answer with a thundering, low-pitched buzz. Suddenly, they burst out of the nest! The attic is instantly filled with thousands upon thousands of excited wasps, all poised and ready to attack.

For the moment, Abby is blissfully unaware of the impending storm. She strides out the bathroom, passing Mike, who practically knocks her down in his effort to finally have his turn in the bathroom. As she heads into her room, she hears a low drone. Could that be her *stomach* growling? "Whoa," she murmurs. "Shouldn't have skipped breakfast."

Back in her room, the blue and violet outfit is waiting on her bed, just where she left it. "Today is going to be perfect," she says. "And nothing— not even Krista Cook and her new yellow car— is going to ruin it."

At just that moment, the lone wasp flies right by her nose.

Yikes! How did that creature get in her room? Abby lets out a small, sharp shriek, and waves it away. Her terrified gaze follows the wasp's path until she sees it fly up to the air conditioning vent. A strange, ominous rumble fills the room and then an entire swarm of wasps bursts out of the vent. Wasps! And so many of them! They fill the room like an evil black cloud. Abby is momentarily frozen and then all at once, her survival instinct kicks in and she runs shrieking from the room, then from the house and from the mass of buzzing, stinging invaders.

Still in her bunny slippers and jammies, Abby stands with her brother and parents on their front sidewalk. They are all wearing white beekeeper's hoods - big white helmets that are shrouded by nets. The Bugs-B-Gone van is parked at the curb behind them. Neighbors start to poke their heads out of windows and gather around; everyone is staring at the Jensen house. By now, the whole place is enveloped by the swarm, with wasps flying crazily in and out of every window on both floors.

Celeste, wearing her Bugs-B-Gone exterminator's jumpsuit and beekeeper's hood, marches briskly out of the house. She strides up to the family and takes the hood off. Following her lead, the Jensens do the same.

"Well, it's a major infestation," says Celeste. "Probably been building for, oh, sixteen years, by the looks of it."

"How long will it take to get them out?" asks Abby's dad. Clearly, he is worried.

"Several days. A year at the most." Celeste sounds mighty

cheery for someone delivering such glum news.

"A *year?!*" exclaims Abby's mom.

Celeste nods, perkily. Then she holds The List out to Abby. "Oh, I managed to save this," she says. Abby grabs it and presses it to her. Could this day get any worse? She looks around to see still more neighbors gathering. They look at the house and then at the Jensens. Abby feels so embarrassed by all this unwanted attention; she wishes she could find somewhere to hide until this mess has been cleaned up.

"This can't be happening. Not to me. Not today," she says. She is near tears. Suddenly, she has an idea and turns to her father. "Daddy, I left some clothes in my gym locker. Please please please drive me to school--"

BBBBBUUUUUUZZZZZZZ! The sound of the wasps makes her stop. She looks up to see a whole chunk of the swarm as it breaks off and flies toward the driveway, completely enveloping the minivan and the car. Abby and her mother gasp. Mike grins, thinking it's way cool.

"I don't think so, pumpkin," says her father in a small voice.

Before Abby can answer, she hears that car horn again, the one she'll no doubt be hearing in her dreams. She looks over to see Krista Cook in her brand new car, smoothly backing out of her driveway. Mike takes off running and stops the car in the street. He leans over and says a few quick words to Krista, who nods and says, "Get in." Then he runs around and buckles himself into the passenger seat. Krista flashes Abby a big, triumphant grin and guns the engine. The car peels off down the street.

"Great!" Abby says loudly. "I'll just take the bus.

By *myself. On my birthday!*"

Her parents look on helplessly as she stomps off toward the bus stop. Stepping off the curb, Abby accidently plunges her foot into a big puddle. She looks down, and then pulls one soaking wet bunny slipper up out of the puddle. The formerly white bunny slipper is now a muddy brown. "Oh. That's just perfect."

She angrily continues down the street, the drenched bunny slipper making a loud *squish, squish* sound with every step she takes. Clutched in her hand is her Birthday Wish List— all the wonderful things that were supposed to happen today. Hah. The joke, it seems, is on her.

At the bus stop, Abby holds up the drenched bunny slipper, letting it drain onto the sidewalk.

"You look pathetic," says a familiar male voice.

Abby looks up to see Jay Kepler, her best friend. Jay is the kid in the photograph in her room; he's taller now but still has the same goofy smile.

"Thanks, Jay. Nice to know I can count on you to state the obvious." She sighs, a long and heartfelt sigh.

"Sorry about your house," Jay says.

"How'd you know?" asks Abby.

"Krista texted the entire junior class."

"That's just peachy." She sighs again. Could this day get any worse?

Jay just looks at her for a second. Then he takes off his jacket and puts it around Abby's shoulders. She doesn't exactly smile, but she does look a shade less miserable. When she puts her hands in the pockets, she feels a small box tied with a bow. She takes it out and looks questioningly at Jay.

"Happy birthday?" he says tentatively.

"Not really," Abby says. So far, this has been the unhappiest birthday she can ever remember.

"C'mon," coaxes Jay. "Open it."

Abby relents and opens the box. Inside she finds one half of a heart-shaped necklace cut in two pieces. She takes it out of the box "It's beautiful, Jay. Where's the other half?"

Sheepishly, Jay digs into his pocket and pulls out his key chain. Attached to it is the other half of the heart. He holds it up next to her necklace. Together, the two halves spell out "BFF."

"Best friends forever," reads Abby. "Aw, Jay. That's sweet. Really sweet."

"You like it?" asks Jay. It's clear he ardently hopes that she does.

"I love it. It's the nicest thing that's happened to me all day," Abby says. She puts on the necklace.

"That bad, huh?"

"Yes!" she bursts out. "I've been planning for this day for eight years." She waves the Wish List in front of his face. "This was supposed to be the day I started acquiring all the wonderful things that come with being a grownup, things like freedom and privacy and respect. But what do I get? Wasps. *Wasps!* Even our backyard is infested! Where am I going to have my Sweet

Sixteen party?"

"You can use my basement," offers Jay.

"Ew! No!" exclaims Abby.

"Right," says Jay, trying not to let his hurt feelings show. "Well, the day's young. Good things could still happen."

"Like what? Like taking the bus? I hate taking the bus," says Abby mournfully. "This is the worst birthday in the history of birthdays."

Jay just stands next to her. He is aching to take her hand in his, but he doesn't dare.

"Today wasn't supposed to be like this," pouts Abby. "Today was supposed to be *magical.*"

Suddenly, out of nowhere, a mail truck screeches up to the curb. Abby and Jay each take a big step back. The truck grinds to a stop in front of them. The mail carrier digs around in the back of the truck for something, flinging packages around in the most alarming way, and finally coming up with a smallish brown box. The carrier leans out the door with the box. With a jolt of surprise, Abby recognizes Celeste, only instead of the exterminator's uniform she had on before, she's wearing a blue postal worker's uniform.

"Abby Jensen?" asks Celeste.

"Yes," Abby answers, wondering what in the world this could be about.

"This is for you." Celeste hands her the package. Then she adds, "Happy Birthday, sweetie!" before starting the engine and speeding off in the mail truck.

Abby and Jay look down at the package. There's no address, no postage. Just her name.

"Don't open it," warns Jay.

"Why?" Abby says. She is curious about what could be inside.

"Real mail is delivered to your house, not your bus stop," says Jay.

"So?"

"It might be a bomb," Jay warns.

"It's not a bomb. It's a birthday present and I'm opening it." Abby is nothing if not stubborn. She rips the box open to find a package of "Sweet Sixteen Birthday Candles" inside. Each candle is numbered 1 through 16. On the back of the box are the directions. She's never seen anything quite like this before.

"Make a wish, light a candle and watch your Sweet Sixteen Birthday Wishes come true," reads Abby with a little snort. "Great. Candles. Not even a stupid gift card."

Jay takes the mailing box and looks inside. "There's something else," he says. He tips the box over and a box of old fashioned matches from the Lucky Duck Chinese Restaurant fall into his hand. Abby grabs the matches out of his hand.

"Hold this," she says, thrusting the list into Jay's hands.

"What are you doing?" he asks.

"Read Wish Number 8," Abby says.

"When I'm sixteen I'll have my own car, preferably red," says Jay, reading from the list.

"I'm lighting one of these candles," says Abby.

"What if something bad happens?" Jay asks.

"What if something *good* happens?" counters Abby. "And besides, if it's a joke, the worst that can happen is we take the bus."

Abby takes out Candle #1, strikes one of the Lucky Duck matches and lights the candle. Then she blows out the match, then the candle. Jay winces, waiting for disaster. But what happens next is not disastrous, but surprising beyond their wildest dreams.

A gleaming silver tour bus speeds out of nowhere and squeals to a stop in front of them. The doors whoosh open and Joey Lockhart emerges from the bus. He wears the same outfit that he was wearing in the poster that hangs in Abby's bedroom. Same adorable hat too. Same adorable expression.

Abby stands there open-mouthed as he comes up to her.

"Are you Abby Jensen?" Joey asks.

"Y-Y-Yes." Abby is so nervous she can't help stuttering.

Joey takes the candles and the matches out of her hands and gives them to Jay. Then the famous international pop star takes her hands in his and kisses her gently on the cheek. Abby is so shocked she can hardly breathe.

"Happy Birthday, Abby," Joey says.

"Thanks." Abby's voice is no more than a squeak.

Joey stands there for another a moment; he seems confused about what he's just done. Shaking his adorable head slightly, he gets back on the bus. The doors whoosh closed and the bus takes off.

Abby and Jay stare after it.

Jay is the first to speak. "What just happened?"

"I've had a crush on him since I was seven," Abby says, marveling. Then it dawns on her. *"When I'm sixteen I'll meet Joey Lockhart."*

"What are you talking about?" asks Jay.

Abby grabs the List and waves it in his face. "It's Wish # 1! Jay! The candles work!"

They hear the roar of a bus engine and look up to see a big yellow school bus headed their way.

"Yeah, but we're still stuck taking the bus."

"Maybe not. I lit Candle # 1 and Wish #1 on the List came true. I think the numbers on the candles correspond with the numbers on my Wish List. Give me # 8!" says Abby with mounting excitement.

Jay hands her Candle #8 along with the box of Lucky Duck matches. As the bus bears down on them, she hastily strikes a match, lights Candle #8, blows out the match, then the candle. All of a sudden, a shiny new red sports car tears down a side street in front of the bus, roars up to Abby and Jay, and stops right in front of them.

"No way!" cries Jay.

"Way way!" Abby cries back. The car, red as a valentine, gleams brightly in the morning sun. The driver opens the door and gets out. Once again, it's Celeste. She's somehow ditched the mail carrier duds and exchanged them for a jaunty chauffeur's outfit and little cap. She waves gaily at the yellow school bus as it rolls on by.

"Gosh, this is fun!" says Celeste.

"I can't believe it! This is my *dream* car!" squeals Abby.

"It's all yours, sweetie," says Celeste as she holds out the keys. "Wanna drive?"

"Yes!" says Abby, reaching for the keys.

But Jay grabs her wrist before her fingers can close around the keys. "No," he says firmly.

"I have my permit," says Abby. "My dad lets me practice in the Hasty Mart parking lot all the time."

"Yeah," snorts Jay. "At *midnight.* When it's *empty.* Abby, when a *total stranger* drives up to you on the street and offers you a *car,* you can't just take it!"

"She's not a total stranger," Abby says. She turns to Celeste. "You look very familiar."

"We're not doing this," Jay says.

"Why not?" Abby wants to know.

"Yeah. Why not?" Celeste echoes.

"Because... you won't have your driver's license until you take the test after school," says Jay, thinking fast.

"Good point," says Celeste. "I'll drive. Get in, you two!"

"Not until you tell us who you are," says Jay.

"I'm Celeste. I'm here to make Abby's Sixteen Wishes come true."

"Oh, that explains pretty much exactly *nothing.*" Jay rolls his eyes.

"C'mon, Jay!" wheedles Abby. "This is the most wonderful, amazing, *magical* thing that's ever happened to me!" She looks him straight in the eye. "Fifty years from now, when you're looking back at your life, don't you want to be able to say you had the guts to get in the car?"

Jay moans. She knows he can't resist a geeky movie reference. She pulls him playfully toward the car. He reluctantly opens Abby's passenger door for her. "I'm going to regret this," he says more to himself than to anyone else.

Abby jumps in the passenger seat, grinning from ear to ear. Celeste adjusts her chauffeur's cap and gets behind the wheel. Jay whimpers a bit, then gets in the back seat. "Just so we're clear, you're some kind of magical being? Like an elf or a fairy?" he asks as he buckles his seatbelt.

"Sure. Why not," says Celeste.

"You don't sound sure," Jay says.

"Jay!" Abby scolds.

"Do you just do birthdays or other events too?" Jay ignores Abby and continues to probe Celeste.

"He babbles when he's nervous," says Abby, hoping Celeste is not offended.

"Why don't you relax, Jay, and enjoy the ride?" says Celeste. "Hold on." With a mischievous grin, she punches the accelerator. Abby and Jay are thrown back against the seats, their hair blown back by some unseen wind. The road behind disappears in a streak of hyper-speed. Abby loves the sensation and laughs out loud. Jay screams. And Celeste lets out a big, long whoop of delight.

Impossibly, only seconds later, the red sports car pulls into the parking lot of their high school. The car slows to a smooth, safe crawl as it enters the busy lot. Abby twists around in her seat to look at Jay. "Wasn't that *awesome?*" she says, clearly elated.

"Have we landed? What does it look like?" he says. Jay's hair is standing up on his head, like it was scared straight. His eyes are squeezed shut.

"What does what look like?" asks Abby.

"Her home planet," croaks Jay.

Celeste looks at him in her rear view mirror. "Sorry, Jay. The only alien planet you'll be visiting today is high school."

The red car pulls into an empty spot. Jay's door flies open and he falls out of the car, kissing the asphalt. "I'll never ditch school again!" he vows.

A crowd of students, including Mike, Logan Buchanan, and his slightly dim-witted best friend, Ted, is gathered around Krista Cook and her new yellow car. Krista is immensely pleased to be the center of all the envious attention. "I already have my driver's license," she brags. "My dad has *connections* at the DMV."

"Yo, Logan. Check out *that* ride," says Ted, spying Abby's new car. Logan turns to see Abby getting out of the red sports car. Unfortunately for her, she is still in her slippers and jammies.

"Hey, Jensen. Did you get new wheels too?" Logan asks. Abby is speechless. Logan Buchanan spoke to her. He really and truly spoke to her. Suddenly, the keys to the red sport scar attached to a sparkly, rhinestone-studded A, are in her hand; they seem to glow magically for a brief second. Abby whips around to look for Celeste but she's gone. She turns back to Logan. "Yes! These are my new wheels…which I bought my-self… for my birthday…which is today." The words tumble out and trip all over each other.

"Cool," says Logan, as if delivering a verdict. Clearly, he is a boy of few words.

Krista's eyes dart back and forth between Abby and Logan. As far as she is concerned, this is all out war.

Abby doesn't see her look. Instead, she focuses on her brother Mike, who rushes up and runs his hands over the sports car. "No way this is yours!" he says.

"What can I say? I'm a saver, not a spender like you," replies Abby.

"Oh, man. I gotta make some bank," Mike says.

Jay gets up off the ground. He looks up toward the front door of the school. Lining the walkway he sees professionally printed campaign signs on wooden stakes that say, "Krista Cook for President. *The ONLY choice.*" He swallows, somehow saddened by the sight. But he says nothing and glances over at Krista, who is busy whispering to a group of her friends, the most popular clique in school, girls so fashion-conscious Abby calls them "The Fashionistas." They all look over at Abby and giggle in a mean, catty way. They start pointing, and several other kids join them.

"Forget to get dressed?" says Krista. "Or is that a new fashion statement?"

Abby looks down at her pink jammies and water-logged bunny slippers. They do look pretty ridiculous next to Krista's designer flats. Before she can even respond, Jay swoops in next to her. "C'mon," he says, taking her by the arm and turning her gently toward school.

"What are you doing?" asks Abby.

"Saving you from more humiliation."

But Abby shakes off the mean girls' remarks. Who cares about them anyway? "I'm not humiliated," she says to Jay. "This is going to be the best birthday *ever!*"

Abby looks at Jay and reads from the List, *"When I'm sixteen I'll have the best Sweet Sixteen Party ever.* If these candles keep working like this, my party is going to be sick." She spins around giddily, and then proclaims to the assembled crowd: "Party tonight at my house! You're all invited!" Everyone— especially Krista and her mean clique of Fashionista friends- bursts out laughing as they part in two streams around her to enter the school. They act as if the idea of her party is just about the most ridiculous thing ever.

"Is it a *pajama* party?" Krista says, and they laugh even harder. Abby looks down at her foolish get-up. She needs some real clothes, and she needs them now. Jay hurries Abby inside and down the hall just as the bell rings. "Just go find yourself some real clothes to wear," says Jay. "I'll make excuses for you. I'll tell Mrs. Hackle you got a leg cramp."

"Thanks, Jay," Abby says gratefully. He ducks into a classroom as Abby continues down the hall in her bunny slippers. When she reaches the girls' locker room, she is relieved to find a pair of jeans and a clean T-shirt. She reaches back inside the locker, hunting for the brightly-colored sneakers she knows she stashed last Thursday. Got 'em! She sniffs gingerly— and then gags. These babies belong in the trash with the ruined bunny slippers, not in her locker. But what will she do for shoes right now? Krista Cook probably has a whole shoe wardrobe in her locker. Then it hits her. She looks down at the List. Wish Number 2. *When I'm sixteen I'll have the cutest clothes in the school.* Abby flashes back to the moment she made the wish. She was eight, and dreamed of strutting down the hall of the high school in oversized sunglasses, a short hot pink skirt, black knee-high boots and huge chandelier earrings. In her fantasy, all her friends line the hall, nodding and applauding. One of the most popular girls in school runs up and hands her a gi-normous gold trophy that says *CUTEST CLOTHES*! Now wouldn't *that* have been cool? Shaking her head to clear the memory, Abby takes out her magic candles and her Lucky Duck matches. She looks around and sits down on the bench.

Abby does not see Krista enter the locker room. Krista has just made sure that her glossy, professionally printed "VOTE 4 KRISTA!" posters are hung all over the school. In fact, just to annoy Abby, she even hired Abby's brother Mike to hang them.

Krista tapes up a "VOTE 4 KRISTA!" poster in the locker room. Then an odd sound catches her attention. She creeps silently around a row of lockers to watch as Abby lights one of the Lucky Duck matches and touches the flame to the wick of Candle #2. But the candle does not light. Abby blows out the match and tries a second time. Still, the candle will not light.

Abby is confused. What's going on here? She is also utterly oblivious to the fact that she is being spied on by Krista whose expression becomes both smug and self-righteous as she backs out of the locker room. Frantically, Abby tries another match, and another. The darned candle just won't light!

Suddenly, Abby looks up to see the not-so-pleasant face of Miss Duffy, the gym teacher, looming over her. Uh oh! Being caught lighting matches in the locker room is definitely not cool.

"Miss Duffy," says Abby in a tiny, scared voice.

"Jensen," Miss Duffy says sternly. She blows out the match and straightens up, her imposing form towering over Abby. "I'll take those," she adds, holding out her hand. Meekly, Abby surrenders the candles and the Lucky Duck matches. Then she glumly follows Miss Duffy out of the gym and down the hall until they reach the office of the school's guidance counselor.

Miss Duffy instructs her to wait there until she is summoned. Abby fidgets, trying not to breathe in the odor from her smelly sneakers. After a few long, dreary minutes, the school's counselor appears, and to Abby's surprise— and great relief— she turns out to be Celeste, who is ushering Logan's friend Ted out of the office. "Keep up the good work, Theodore, and you'll be president one day," she says.

"You think so?" Ted asks. Hope paints his handsome, dumb face.

"Absolutely," Celeste says with utter sincerity.

Ted walks off, proudly as Abby, amazed, looks on. "So, you can tell the future too?" she asks Celeste. "I mean, you really think Ted is going to be president some day?"

"No," says Celeste. "I don't. But it gave Ted hope. C'mon in." She walks back into the office. Once inside, Abby plops, dejectedly in a chair while Celeste perches on the edge of the table. "What's up, sweetie?" she asks. With her cocked head and bright, sparkling eyes, she looks like a little bird.

"What's up? You know what's up. That's why you're here pretending to be the counselor. Why didn't that stupid candle light?" She gives Celeste a beseeching look.

"Because of the Rules," says Celeste.

"The Rules?" says Abby. Like that's supposed to explain anything?

"You mean you don't know about the Rules?" Celeste says.

"What are you talking about?" says Abby. This conversation is about as clear as mud.

"The candles are magic and all magic has rules. One candle and one wish per hour. You lit Candle Number 1 at 7:58 this morning and Joey Lockhart showed up. Then you lit Candle Number 8 at precisely 8:00 a.m. Your wishes were two minutes apart, but within different hours."

"So now I have to wait…"

"--twenty-seven minutes--" supplies Celeste.

"--before I can make another wish," finishes Abby. "Great." Her tone drips sarcasm. "You could have printed that on the box. Any other magic candle rules I should know about?"

"Only one," says Celeste, "but it's a doozy. The magic in the candles expires at midnight tonight, so no more wishes after then. Oh, and all the wishes you've made become permanent."

"Permanent at midnight," Abby repeats, wanting to be sure she gets it straight.

"Yup."

"So at midnight, that gorgeous car out there is mine forever," says Abby.

"Absolutely," confirms Celeste.

"And in twenty-six and a half minutes, I'll have cuter clothes than Krista Cook." Now there is something worth waiting for.

"Yeah. She really can't stand you," says Celeste.

"You know about that?"

"I really shouldn't do this, but..." Celeste reaches behind her and takes out a plastic box labeled LOST & FOUND. After a moment or two of digging, she pulls out a yellow diary. Metallic butterflies flutter across the cover, which reads *KRISTA COOK'S PERSONAL DIARY*. As Celeste hands it to Abby, the cover emits a magical shimmer. "Read for yourself."

"Oh, I couldn't," says Abby, looking down at the diary.

"Well…maybe just a page or two."

"I suggest 10, 23 and 37," says Celeste, conspiratorially, handing her back the box of magic candles and matches. "And be a little more careful where you light those puppies." Then she opens the door and gently shoves Abby out.

Walking through the crowded hallway, Abby ignores the milling sea of bodies around her; she is totally engrossed in reading the diary. Quickly, she flips through the pages, becoming more and more agitated as she does. She is so preoccupied that she doesn't see Jay approaching and crashes right into him.

"Good stuff?" Jay asks, pointing to the diary.

"You have no idea." Abby slams the diary shut. She glares at Krista, who stands next to a voting table. The Fashionistas, all decked out in designer outfits, are writing in their votes and tucking them in a ballot box that sits on the table. Mike is at the table too, handing out 4 x 6 printed cards.

"Thanks for voting for me!" Krista says to anyone and everyone passing by.

Abby marches right up to her. "Krista, I know you've loathed me since we were eight years old, but I didn't know--" she holds up the diary "--you've been keeping score!"

"Where did you get that?" demands Krista.

"From the Birthday Fairy," Abby says snidely.

"Right," Krista shoots back, just as snidely. She grabs for the diary. "Give it to me!"

Abby holds the diary away from her and continues, revealing what she just read. "When we were ten, I had my first sleepover. You decided to have one too... and paid everybody to come to yours."

Krista grabs for the diary again. "You have no right to read that. It's *mine.*"

"Then why is it all about *me?*" Abby retorts. For the first time, Krista's friends look at her like she may not be so cool. And for the first time, Krista Cook is embarrassed. Sensing her opponent's weakness, Abby, goes on. "When we were twelve, I entered the school talent show with my baton twirling act, so you entered too— *juggling twelve batons!* Every year, you competed with me and every year you won." She stares directly into Krista's eyes. "You've tortured me since the third grade. Can't you just give it a rest?"

"Don't play innocent with me," Krista spits back. "You know what you did." She grabs the diary and holds it tightly. "And for *this,* I'm going to make sure nobody comes to your party." She hands Abby one of the 4 x 6 cards.

"What's this?" Abby asks.

"An invitation to my Sweet Sixteen Party tonight," says Krista smugly. *"Everybody's* going to be there. Now, if you'll excuse me, I've got some campaigning to do."

Jay picks up a voting ballot from the table. He looks up at

Krista, a sad look on his face. "You don't need to campaign, Krista. You're the only name on the ballot."

"Well, then. I'm sure to win," gloats Krista.

"Why are you doing this?" asks Jay. "You're not even interested in student government."

"And you are?" demands Krista.

Jay shrugs. "Well... I..." he stutters.

"I didn't *think* so," says Krista tartly as she turns away from him.

"I'd love to be Student Body President," says Jay meekly. But not a soul hears him. Not even Abby.

Krista waves happily to someone behind Abby. Abby turns to see Logan striding toward them, followed by Ted. Logan passes Abby without a word and walks up to Krista. "Hey, Krista. Somebody said you needed help."

"Hand these out for me?" Krista hands him a box of VOTE 4 KRISTA buttons.

"Sure," Logan says.

"Thanks, Logan," says Krista, giving him a hug. Behind his back and over his shoulder, she mouths to Abby, "He's mine."

Abby whips around, turning away from Krista and Logan. "She's doing it. She's ruining my birthday. *Again,*" she says to Jay.

"Don't let her get to you," Jay says.

"You're right, Jay. I'm going to put an end to her reign of terror..." She pauses to look up at the clock on the wall. It says 9:00 a.m. "... right about now."

Abby looks around for someplace to go, someplace private. She sees a door marked "Supply Closet." Perfect. She takes off toward it. Jay, watching her, is totally puzzled.

Abby steps inside the spacious supply room and flips on a dim yellowish light. Surrounded by racks of school supplies, mops, buckets and broom, she checks to make sure there's nothing flammable. Then she takes the Wish List, the candles and the Lucky Duck matches out of her bag. Carefully, she lights Candle #2 and recites from the List: *When I'm sixteen, I'll have the cutest clothes in school.* She blows out the match and the candle, and suddenly her eyes widen to see that the supply room has been magically transformed into the most fabulous, humongous walk-in closet ever. It's filled with beautiful designer clothes, glorious handbags and incredible shoes. Everything is totally organized and color coordinated. Celeste is there too, wearing a very chic yellow tunic and glam gold necklace. She's looking and sounding a lot like an editor at a major fashion magazine. "Hi-hi!" she greets Abby.

"Celeste, it's beautiful!" Abby exclaims.

"I know, right? I've been waiting for you to make this wish," says Celeste gleefully. "I just love shopping. Especially when it's *free!*"

"I don't even know where to start," says Abby.

"That's what I'm here for," Celeste says, and then goes to work, pulling out dresses, skirts and tops for Abby to try, adjusting her collar, straightening a sleeve or smoothing a hem.

"Ever since the third grade, whatever I did, Krista did better," says Abby as Celeste works her magic. "She's never satisfied unless she's winning and I'm losing. But today I decided she's not going to make me miserable anymore. I have a plan and this wish is the first part."

"Would you say Krista Cook always has the cutest clothes in school?" asks Celeste.

"And shoes and handbags," Abby adds.

Celeste steps back, satisfied. "Not anymore." She grins at Abby, who grins right back.

When Abby emerges from the supply room, she has been totally transformed.

Her pink designer dress, cropped brocade jacket, faux flower pin and cluster of beads are all super cute, trendy yet totally appropriate for high school. She looks like a Top Teen Model.

The Fashionistas, on their way to their next class, see her and do a double take. They squeal and rush over to her.

"That top is *not* an original You-Know-Who, is it?" one of them asks.

"It is," says Abby proudly.

"Shut. Up," says another.

"Oh! Those shoes are to die for," exclaims the first Fashionista, cheerfully adding, "I hate you."

"Wanna have lunch near us?" asks her friend.

"Sure," says Abby.

"Yay!" says the most fashionable Fashionista. "I just want to *sit* next to that handbag."

"*This* handbag?" calls Krista. They all turn to look; Krista strolls up to them, holding up the same champagne handbag as Abby is holding. "I got it for my birthday... *last* year," she gloats. "You're not all that, Jensen," she adds.

"Yoo-hoo, Abby!" calls Celeste. Abby turns to see Celeste coming out of the supply room with a different, even more fabulous faux-croc eggplant colored handbag. "I am so sorry. Give me that old thing." Abby and Celeste exchange handbags. "This one's so hot, it's not even out yet," adds Celeste.

"Thank you so much," cries Abby. They air kiss twice, like a pair of European fashion models, and Celeste heads back toward the supply room.

"I'll just ship the rest of the collection to you when the wasp infestation is over!" Celeste jubilantly calls out over her shoulder. "Auf Wiedersehen!" She disappears into the supply room. Like a herd of stampeding shoppers at a bargain sale, the Fashionistas shove past Abby and follow Celeste to the Supply Closet. They grapple and shove each other to get inside. Abby giggles as she watches them thinking, they look like a flock of pecking, honking geese. Then she becomes aware of Krista and is startled by the look of disgust on her face.

"I know what you're doing and it's not going to work," Krista snarls.

"I'm just having the best birthday of my entire life," says Abby, brightly, overjoyed to realize she finally got to Krista.

"Well, good luck with that, 'cause it's not over yet." Krista stalks off, passing the supply closet just the Fashionistas stumble out. They all carry mops, buckets and brooms and look anything *but* fashionable.

7

In the girls' locker room, Miss Duffy blows her whistle—loudly. All the girls quiet down at the sound of it. "Everybody on the track in five," says Miss Duffy. Now the silence is replaced by groans all around, from everybody, that is, except Krista. She's still to busy brooding about how Abby humiliated her. Abby comes into the locker room with her new eggplant colored handbag in time to see their pained expressions. She looks at Krista and seizes another opportunity.

"Late again, Jensen," says Miss Duffy in a clipped voice.

"Yes, Miss Duffy, I am late," says Abby in a sweet-as-sugar tone. "I'm late because…" she pauses. "I went back to my locker for *this.*" Abby holds up the new handbag. She can see a slight beading of sweat break out on Miss Duffy's forehead. Is she actually licking her lips?

"Oh, I see. It's no excuse for tardiness, but that is a *beautiful* bag."

"It's for you," Abby says, offering it to Miss Duffy.

"For me?" Miss Duffy squeaks.

"I was saving it for your Christmas present, but look, it matches your track suit perfectly."

"It actually does." Miss Duffy looks down at her lavender velour tracksuit and then back at the bag.

"Happy Monday," Abby says, holding out the bag.

"Happy Monday to me," says Miss Duffy, giddily. Her hands shake slightly as she accepts the bag. Miss Duffy is suddenly in a *much* better mood. Without taking her eyes off her new hand-bag, she speaks to class. "Instead of running killer laps, let's just play a friendly game of volleyball."

As soon as these words leave her lips, the class lets out exclamations of happiness. Abby grins and walks down the row of lockers, passing a scowling Krista and getting low-fives and fist bumps all the way down the row.

Back out in the gym, the teams get ready to play. It's a co-ed gym class, so the teams are mixed: boys and girls together. Krista is the leader of one team that consists of a bunch of very fit, trim girls all decked out in matching volleyball uniforms. They look like professional teen athletes. In contrast, Jay leads the other team: regular students wearing a hodgepodge of mis-matched gym clothes.

Great, thinks Jay. *We're really going to score with this motley crew.* It turns out they are one player short. He pleads with Miss Duffy, who's busy petting her new handbag, to let Abby play on his team.

"C'mon. We need her," he entreats.

"JENSEN! Get out here!" yells Miss Duffy.

Abby, still in the locker room, jumps at the sound of her name. But before she hurries onto the court, she lights a Lucky Duck match. Wish #12 is what is on her agenda. *When I'm sixteen, I'll beat Krista Cook at something, anything, everything."* In a rush, she puts the match to candle #12 and then *Boom!*

The door swings open and Abby makes her entrance like a Teen Vogue model at a sports fashion shoot. Everyone turns to stare as she struts across the gym floor in her brand new shorts, matching top and sweatshirt. Her sneakers are brand new as well, and look like the latest in athletic style. Her sharp outfit matches her obvious confidence in her looks and ability to finally beat Krista Cook.

Miss Duffy, cuddling her designer handbag, blows her whistle. "Play ball!" she shouts.

The teams square off. Krista is at the net ready to attack. Abby is on the other side, right in Krista's face. Jay sidles up to her. "You sure about this?" he asks quietly.

"Why shouldn't I be sure?" asks Abby.

"Because you're the least athletic person I know."

"Not anymore. I got the birthday mojo," Abby says. She doesn't even see Krista, who spikes the ball toward her face.

"Duck!" cries Jay.

Fortunately, Abby ducks and covers in the nick of time. The ball whizzes by her head. Miss Duffy, handbag over her shoulder, blows her whistle. "One, zip," she announces.

"You *tried* to hit me!" Abby says to Krista.

"It's called *spiking*. It's how you *win*," says Krista.

Abby looks at her. *Okay,* she thinks. *If she wants to play rough, we're gonna play rough. Let's see how she likes a taste of her own medicine.*

Krista's team serves again. Abby watches the ball sail right over her head. Behind her, another player bumps the ball. Jay sets it and the ball arcs high over Abby's head. This time, Abby jumps, a supernaturally high, magic-infused leap in the air. As the heels of her shoes leave the ground, they emit that special shimmer.

From high over the net, Abby spikes the ball down on Krista. Krista looks up as the volleyball rockets toward her. It lands with a *thunk!* squarely in the middle of her forehead. Her eyes cross and she slumps to the floor. She's out cold, so she doesn't see the other students hoist Abby on their shoulders, nor does she hear their cries of "MVP! MVP! MVP!"

A little while later, Krista is lying on an exam table in the nurses' office, an ice pack resting on her forehead. She can still hear the chants in her memory, taunting her. "M.V.P! M.V.P.!" Krista sits up, suddenly. The chanting voices fade away. The door opens and Celeste comes in, now dressed in a nurse's uniform. "Look who's awake! How're you feelin'?"

Krista's hand goes to her forhead where she got thumped with the volleyball. "Um, fine. I had a weird nightmare,"

"No, honey. That was real," Celeste replies, matter-of-factly. "Abby Jensen creamed you. Oh, and you're wanted in the Principal's office."

Befuddled, Krista gets off the table, hands Celeste the ice pack and opens the door. She walks down the hall, a little less confidently than usual.

In the principal's office, she finds Abby, still in her trendy gym clothes, chatting and laughing with Mr. Smith, school principal. It looks like they are best buds. What is *this* all about? Krista wonders. The Student Body President Ballot Box sits open on the counter. Krista is instantly suspicious.

"You wanted to see me, Mr. Smith?" she asks.

"Yes. Big news, Cook. The election is over."

"How can it be over? A lot of people haven't voted yet," Krista says.

"Nope, they ALL voted," Mr. Smith says. "We had a one hundred percent voter turn-out." He high-fives Abby. She grins.

"What's going on here?" Krista asks.

Instead of answering, Mr. Smith takes the microphone for the school sound system and jauntily flips the switch. "Good morning, students," he says, voice amplified by the loudspeaker.

"I am pleased to announce the winner of the most votes for Student Body President is...ABBY JENSEN!"

In the packed hallway, students, including Jay, Mike, Logan and Ted, stop and look up at the speakers. Everyone, except Jay, who's totally mystified, cheers and applauds. He alone looks around him, thinking that the whole world has gone nuts.

Back in the office, Abby beams. Krista goes very still. She can't believe Abby won. Now Abby takes the microphone. "I want to thank all of you who voted for me and made this dream possible--" she says over the loudspeaker. But Krista violently yanks the microphone away. "It's not possible!" She grabs a handful of ballots from the open ballot box. "She wasn't even on the ballot!" Her voice sounds desperate.

Mr. Smith tries to pry the microphone from her tightly clenched fingers. "Alrighty, if you would just let go," he says. A high-pitched *squeal* comes from the speakers. Everyone covers their ears and winces. Mr. Smith switches off the microphone. "Abby was a write in," he tells Krista gently. Krista looks at one of the crumpled ballots in her hand. Krista's name is crossed out and "ABBY J" is handwritten on it with a box and a checkmark next to her name. *All* of the ballots are like that.

"Better luck next time, Krista," says Abby, brightly. Hah! *For once,* she has beaten Krista and boy, does it feel good! Abby walks out of Mr. Smith's office, leaving a silent and stunned Krista behind.

In the hallway, Abby is surrounded by a crush of students. Everyone wants to shake her hand, pat her on the back or offer congratulations. Jay is there too, but she walks past him. He looks over at the door to Mr. Smith's office. Krista is standing there, alone and forlorn, devastated by having lost to Abby. He actually feels a little sorry for her. Then he shakes off the feeling and hurries off to the chem lab. He has a free period and a lot of work to do for extra credit.

Once he reaches the lab, Jay dons his safety goggles and starts to work on his chemistry experiment. Abby is supposed to meet him here but she has not arrived yet. Well, no wonder. With all the new-found magic in her life, she barely has time for him any more. Even though he is supposed to be working on his lab experiment, Jay pulls out his notebook and begins to doodle. He draws a sign stuck into a lawn; on the sign are the words *Jay Kepler for Student Body President*. Over and over again he traces the words, even if no one is ever going to see them.

Abby rushes into the chemistry classroom to meet Jay. She is flushed with the thrill of victory. She's changed back into the cute outfit Celeste picked for her earlier that day.

"Ha!" she crows. "I finally beat Krista Cook!"

Jay keeps working without looking up. "You had a little help," he says finally.

"I know! Isn't it amazing? This day just keeps getting better and better!"

"For you," he mutters.

"What did you say?"

"Nothing," Jay says. He is not in the mood to repeat himself. She wouldn't care anyway, he thinks. "Can we just do this experiment? We both need the extra credit."

"Nah. I'll just give the teacher some strappy sandals and a pashmina--"

Jay suddenly turns on her. "No!' he says with feeling. "Just... give it a rest, okay?"

"What's wrong with you?" Abby is stunned. Jay has never yelled at her before.

"I don't know. This whole wish thing. You're changing too fast, Abby. I can't keep up," Jay says.

"What do you mean?" She is genuinely puzzled.

"You've always been allergic to volunteer work, and now all of a sudden you're Student Body President?"

"Being president is, like, an honor," says Abby.

"No. Being president is an important job. It should go to someone who really wants it."

"Like who?" she challenges. "Krista?"

"No." Jay discretely closes his notebook so Abby won't see what he was drawing.

"Well, I'm sure I'll do just fine," says Abby. "I'll have you to help me."

Jay just shakes his head. "C'mon, don't be like that," she coaxes. "The people spoke, and the people voted for me."

"The candles spoke," he says sourly.

Abby realizes she has to do something to get Jay out of his bad mood. "You can't be mad at me," she says, finally.

"Why not?"

"Because it's my birthday." She waits, but Jay says nothing. She tries a different angle. "Because you're my best friend." Still no reply. She gets a great idea and whips out a little green card that says, *FREE LUNCH CARD*. "Because as Student Body President, I get free lunch. Every day."

"No way!" Jay finally exclaims.

"*Way* way!" she replies. "Now take off your goofy glasses and let your commander-in-chief buy you a sandwich."

He looks at her. She's just so cute in her designer outfit, that amazing smile, her cute turned up nose. He gives in just a little. "What kind of sandwich?"

"Any kind you want!" Abby grins happily and turns to open the door, only to find a crowd of students are jammed right outside, waiting for her. They start snapping cell phone pix of her, clamoring like crazed paparazzi pursuing a celebrity.

"Abby! Over here!" calls one student. "Abby, I love you!" cries another.

Shocked, Jay slams the door in their faces. "What did you do now?" he demands. "Wish # 10," says Abby. *When I'm sixteen, I'll be popular.* I wrote it one night when I was tired of feeling invisible. I fantasized that I was dressed like a movie star, in a sequined dress and a fake fur wrap. I dreamed about signing autographs for all my screaming fans. Even Joey Lockhart would be there, asking me to sign a picture for him!" Abby looks off, momentarily lost in the memory. "I loved that wish," she adds, returning to the present.

"Right," says Jay, clearly unimpressed. He opens the door and faces the crowd. "Come on, people. Make a hole." He takes Abby by the hand and pulls her out into the throng.

After they get their free food, Abby and Jay sit on the hood of her red sports car sharing a sandwich and some fruit. Krista's new yellow car is right next to them. Abby and Jay are both watching something the Fashionistas are up to at a nearby picnic table.

"Look at them. I don't have to do a thing," Abby explains. "Just show up."

"They're planning your birthday party?" Jay says. "The whole, entire thing?"

"Yep."

Together, Abby and Jay continue to watch the Fashionistas. One of them is standing at an easel on which a white board is perched. At the top is written:

ABBY JENSEN'S SWEET SIXTEEN PARTY

Under the title, someone has drawn a detailed architectural rendering of what looks like a tree-lined street in Paris.

"Their dads are business partners. Apparently, they own half of Vegas. They're throwing my party at one of their hotels," says Abby.

"Abs," Jay says. "I don't mean to rain on your birthday parade, but Vegas? That's not really your style."

"And your basement is?" Abby says.

"Hey, I have foosball," he says, mocking defensively.

"Good point. But this is my one and only Sweet Sixteen Party. I want it to be spectacular." Suddenly, she gasps. "I don't have anything to wear!"

Abby and Jay are so engrossed in their conversation that they don't realize Krista has been slumped down at the wheel of her yellow car, eavesdropping. When she is sure they are not looking, she carefully straightens up again.

"We both have a free period right now. Let's go buy you a

dress," says Jay.

Abby is at first excited; then she wilts. "I can't. The wasps are holding my party money hostage."

"I'll spot you the cash," Jay offers.

"You would do that?" Abby asks.

"Sure," Jay says. What he doesn't say is that he would do anything for her. And not just because they're best friends.

"Jay, you're the best," says Abby. Together, they jump up and hop into the car. But once inside, Abby sits motionless at the wheel. The Wish List, Candles and Lucky Duck matches are on the dashboard. "We can't go," she says. "I don't have my driver's license yet."

Jay snatches the wish list off the dashboard. He begins to read aloud. "Wish Number Seven: *When I'm sixteen, I'll get my driver's license*". Abby grins and holds out her hand. Jay hands her the Lucky Duck matches and holds up Candle #7.

Krista, who is still in her car, strains to get a glimpse at what Abby is doing. When tires screech behind her, she spins around to see a car with a DMV medallion on the door pulling into the parking lot, squealing to a stop behind Abby's red sports car.

A man gets out the car. He's wearing a white short-sleeved shirt with a pocket protector and holds a clipboard. It looks like he is DMV employee. He strides up to the driver's window of the red sports car and knocks. Abby powers down her window. The man wrinkles his forehead and consults his clipboard.

"Abigail Louise Jensen?" he asks.

"Yes."

He looks around, confused. "This is highly unusual," he mutters.

"Can I help you?" asks Abby.

He reluctantly hands her a laminated card. Abby takes it. She looks down to see that it is a driver's license that says "Abigail Louise Jensen" with her photo on it and everything. Abby gasps, and shows the card to Jay. "My driver's license!" she sings out.

"And there ya go," Jay says.

"Thank you so much!" Abby says to the man. He frowns, turns and walks back to the DMV car. He climbs in the passenger seat, brow still furrowed.

"Oh, lighten up, Harry," says a woman's voice from the driver's seat. Seated at the wheel is Celeste, also wearing a short-sleeved shirt with a pocket protector, only on her, it looks adorable. "You needed to get out of that cubicle anyway," she says.

"But we really don't do this kind of thing," says Harry.

"I know. But wasn't it fun?"

"My cubicle was fun," says Harry, still perplexed.

Celeste giggles and drives the DMV car out of the parking lot. Abby's red sports car pulls out after it.

"Jay?" Abby begins.

"Yes, Abs," he says.

"This is now, officially, the best sixteenth birthday in the history of sixteenth birthdays," says Abby. She does not see that Krista's yellow car has pulled out right after her. Krista is following them.

Abby's new car handles like a dream and after about fifteen minutes, Abby parks in front of an upscale boutique. She and Jay get out of the car. Jay looks at the fancy store front and all the expensive-looking clothes in the window. "Abby, you can't afford a hanger here," he says.

"Not true. Since I don't have to pay for my own party, I'm spending every penny I saved on the perfect dress." She can't wait to go inside and pick it out. But what color should she go for? Pink is pretty but too predictable. How about black? Red? Silver? No, a crazy pattern, that's what she'll look for. Zebra stripes or flowers or dots. Something no other girl— and certainly not Krista— will think to wear. Abby is so absorbed in her plans that she doesn't even notice Krista's yellow car pulling up across the street. Neither does Jay.

Krista gets out of the car and waits across the street, hiding behind a mail box. When she is sure that Jay and Abby have their backs toward her, she starts across the street.

Jay pulls his wallet out of his jeans pocket and checks it for cash. He hopes there is enough. Whew. He's got several bills.

He goes to put it back in his pocket just as Abby yanks him into the store. Neither he nor Abby notice that the wallet drops to the pavement, flopping open as it does. But Krista notices and, after Jay and Abby have gone into the boutique, she picks it up. Clutching the lost wallet in her hands, a mean little smile settles on her face.

When Abby walks into the boutique, a snooty saleswoman peers at her over her half-glasses. Abby, busy going through a rack of party dresses, ignores her. Jay settles into an upholstered chair in the middle of the room, attempting to look cool, but feeling incredibly awkward.

"What do you think?" says Abby, holding up a green sequined dress for Jay's approval.

"It's nice," Jay says.

"No. Too disco," Abby decides and puts it back. She selects another dress, holding it up to herself in the mirror. Then she starts humming, her mind awhirl with thoughts of the party and herself in a super gorgeous dress.

Jay watches her. How is it that he has known her for all these years and yet not known her at all? It's like he's just woken up to the fact that she's beautiful and bubbly, funny and smart. That he feels so good when he's near her. He might as well admit, at least to himself: he's crazy about her, and not in a best friend sort of way. He looks over at her now. She holds up a plum colored strapless party dress and turns to him.

"What about this one?"

"You're... it's beautiful," he corrects himself before she's aware of the slip.

"But do you think *Logan* will like it?" Abby wants to know.

"How should I know?" Jay's face falls. *Logan, Logan, Logan*. He never wants to hear the guy's name again.

"Touchy," Abby says, slightly puzzled. Why is he in such a grouchy mood?

"Why don't you just light number sixteen right now and make the stupid wish? Poof. Logan Buchanan is yours."

"It doesn't work that way," she says.

"Uh, yes it does. It's worked that way all day."

"I want Logan to like me for me, not because I put some magic birthday spell on him." She looks at the dress. "I'm trying this on." She reaches into the rack and pulls out a few more dresses. "And these." She heads to the dressing room.

Jay sighs, a deep, defeated sigh. He looks at his watch. They have to get back to school soon; he hopes Abby will hurry.

Outside, Krista drops the wallet into her designer handbag and goes into the boutique. She quietly approaches the counter. She can see Jay nervously waiting for Abby.

Just then, Abby comes out of the dressing room in the plum colored party dress and examines herself in the three-way mirror. Krista quickly steps to the counter and puts on a huge pair of sunglasses.

"I'll take these," Krista says to the Saleswoman, taking out her own wallet to pay. "I really feel for you," she adds. "Wasting your time on *kids* like that."

"A customer's a customer," the Saleswoman replies.

"Oh, trust me. They won't be buying anything," Krista says knowingly. The mean little smile returns to her face.

The Saleswoman looks over at Abby and Jay. *Maybe this girl is right. Maybe they are just kids playing around in my store.*

"Look, Jay. It's perfect, isn't it?" Abby says.

"Sure," he says, wishing they could leave already.

"Well, I love it and I think Logan's going to love it too."

"Good. Sold. Can we go now?"

Abby twirls in front of Jay, trying to playfully get him out of his bad mood. The Saleswoman marches over to them. *This has gone on long enough,* she thinks. She'll end this once and for all.

"I'm sorry. This is a store, not a playground," the saleswoman says in a frosty tone.

"Exactly," says Jay.

"I like this one," Abby says.

"I'm sure you do. Why don't you *kids* just come back with your parents?" says the saleswoman.

"We're not *kids*. I'm *sixteen*," huffs Abby.

"Congratulations," says the saleswoman. Her sarcasm is so thick you could cut it with a knife. "Give me the dress," she orders.

"No, we're buying it! Jay, show her your money," says Abby.

Jay reaches back for his wallet. It's not there. He pats his other rear pocket. No wallet. He's beginning to get worried. Next he pats his front pockets. Nothing. Okay, now it's official: he's not worried, he's panicked. "My wallet--" he says. But no more words will come.

The saleswoman grabs Jay roughly by the sleeve. "You," she commands. "Out."

"Hey! You can't do that!" Abby objects.

"Watch me," the saleswoman replies.

"But we're *customers!*" pleads Abby.

"No, you're *children*. Get that dress off, *now,*" says the Saleswoman.

Jay leaves the store while Abby, furious, storms back to the dressing room. She flops down on a tufted velvet ottoman, pouting. There is a clock on the wall and she stares at it as the hands move from 12:59 to 1:00. Suddenly, she knows just what to do. She digs the box of Birthday Candles and Lucky Duck matches out of her handbag. She carefully chooses Candle #9. *When I'm sixteen, people will stop treating me like a kid.* Now this is an important wish; she can remember the moment she made it perfectly and suddenly she's in the memory.

She is fourteen and already humiliated by a set of braces that make her look awful. Her parents are having a dinner party for some neighbors, including Krista and her parents. Abby is stuck at the Kids' Table, while Krista gets to dine with the adults. The kids eat goopy sugary cupcakes and play with party favors like silly string and rolled-up paper noise-makers. The chairs are so small, Abby's knees are practically under her chin. She looks forlornly over at Krista at the adults' table. They're eating chocolate mousse served in champagne glasses. It looks both elegant and delicious. Suddenly, the kid next to Abby plants a cupcake, frosting side up, right into her cheek. To top off her humiliation, silly string flies at her from all sides of the kids' table.

Sitting in the dressing room, Abby burns just thinking about that memory. She quickly lights the candle and makes Wish #9. *"When I'm sixteen, people will stop treating me like a kid."* Then she strides out of the dressing room, wearing the dress she just tried on for Jay. Oddly enough, the dress now feels about two sizes too small. It just fit her a few minutes ago; how weird is that? She tugs on it uncomfortably. The Saleswoman looks up from the counter.

"Where's my friend?" Abby asks. She knew Jay was kicked out of the store but she thought he'd be waiting for her outside. Wrong.

"There was a boy here, but he left with a girl in the cutest little yellow car--" says the woman. She suddenly seems really

"Your first sixteenth birthday picture...
It's going on our family webpage."

16 WISHES

"Well, it's a major infestation...
Oh, I managed to save this."

"Great. Candles.
Not even a stupid gift card."

"What if something good happens?"

"Party tonight at my house! You're all invited!"

"I didn't know you've been keeping score!"

KRISTA **7** | **0** ABBY

16 WISHES

Abby flashes back to
the moment she made the wish.

"I just love shopping.
Especially when it's free!"

"Would you say
Krista Cook always
has the cutest
clothes in school?...
Not anymore."

"I just want to sit next to that handbag."

"When I'm sixteen, I'll beat Krista Cook at something, anything, EVERYTHING."

16 WISHES

"the people spoke, and the people voted for me"

"Oh, trust me. They won't be buying anything."

He's crazy about her, and not in a best friend sort of way.

Jay digs in his
jeans pocket and pulls
out his key ring.
The other half of
the heart with the
letter "F"...

The party represents the best of both Abby and Krista
and the whole thing glows like a jewel in the night.

16WISHES

"It is now, officially, the best sixteenth birthday in the history of sixteenth birthdays!"

friendly.

"He left with *Krista?*"

"It appears so," says the woman. But she is more interested in the dress Abby is wearing than in where Jay went and with whom. "Turn around," commands the woman. Confused, Abby obeys. "That outfit is all wrong. It's far too young for you."

"And it's suddenly really tight, too," adds Abby.

"Let's get you into something more age appropriate." The woman, who is by now positively helpful, pulls three items from the racks. "Try these."

"But I don't have any money," Abby says.

"Oh, we'll just put them on your charge account."

"I have a charge account?!" Abby is surprised, but thrilled. She's always wanted a charge account. When did that happen?

"Are you all right, Miss Jensen?" the woman asks. She seems genuinely concerned.

"Oh yeah. I'm just fine." Abby looks at the candle and grins. Then she whips around gleefully and heads back to the dressing room, grabbing a few more items on her way.

Thirty minutes later, Abby emerges from the boutique looking like a very sophisticated young woman. Her clothes, her high-heeled pumps, her hair and even her makeup all contribute to this impression. No longer a school girl, she seems every bit the successful young professional on a lunch hour shopping spree, her arms laden with several smart bags from the boutique. She is smiling as the saleswomen walks her to the street, though she nearly twists her ankle trying to balance on her killer new heels.

Abby drives her car back to the school lot and parks. She hears the bell ring. Uh oh— she'll be late. She hurries inside and collides with Miss Duffy as she is coming around the corner.

"Sorry, Miss Duffy," says Abby.

"Do we know each other?" Miss Duffy asks.

Is she for real? Abby wonders. Of course they know each other. *This woman has been on her case all year.* But she doesn't want to get in trouble so all she says is "Yeah."

"Hm. You must be the new substitute teacher, which means I don't have to babysit those little monsters." Her face brightens at the thought, but Abby is getting more and more confused. Substitute teacher? What is she talking about? Maybe the collision rattled something in Miss Duffy's brain, because she sure is acting strange.

But Miss Duffy seems to think everything is just dandy. She nods to a nearby classroom door. "They're all yours," she says, and then walks on. Abby watches her go, totally confused.

Abby peeks into the window of the classroom door. She opens the door cautiously. There's no teacher. Several students are working in pairs at lab tables.

She spies Jay, wearing goggles again. He's doing an experiment that involves pouring crystals from a test tube into a beaker of smoky liquid. His partner is a girl, also wearing lab goggles. They're both laughing and having fun together.

"Psssst!" Abby tries to get Jay's attention. Not happening.

Right next to Jay, Logan is working at another lab station. He's pouring blue liquid from one beaker to another. He hears her and looks up. Abby smiles at him. Logan grins back at her... and glops blue liquid all over the lab table. Grossed out by the spill, she refocuses on her task: getting Jay's attention. "Psssst! Jay!" she calls again. Jay and his lab partner are watching a blob of foam bubble up and over the top of their beaker. Jay turns to see Abby. She frantically waves him over. He takes off his goggles.

"I'll be right back," Jay says to his partner. When she takes off her lab goggles, Abby sees that it's Krista. But she seems changed somehow. At first Abby cannot pinpoint the difference. The she gets it: Krista is not gloating or scowling or frowning. Krista looks... *happy*.

"Oh great," she says. "Leave me to wrangle the blob all alone." But she's clearly teasing, because when he pouts, she says, "No, go," with a smile.

Jay grins at her and steps out of class and into the hallway to talk with Abby.

"Yes?" he says, acting very formal.

"What is wrong with you?" Abby says in a hurt voice. Has everyone gone nuts today?

"Excuse me?" Jay says.

"Hello! You *left* me, *stranded,* on my *birthday.* What kind of a best friend does that?"

"Best friend? What are you talking about?" says Jay. It's clear from the red flush spreading all over his face that he is not comfortable having this conversation.

"Oh, okay," Abby says. She doesn't get his little game but she'll play along if it makes him happy. "Hi, my name is Abby Jensen. Have we met?"

"Yeah. A long time ago, I think." It doesn't seem like he's playing.

"Shut up," Abby says, giving him a shove.

He backs away from her, more than a little freaked out.

"Stop it. I'm not your best friend. I'm a sophomore. You're a... *woman*."

"Thank you, but I'm just four months older than you," Abby reminds him.

"Yeah, in dog years." Jay snorts. "Listen, I'm in the middle of an important experiment—"

"And I'm in the middle of an important *birthday!*"

"I'm sorry," he says. "I gotta go."

She grabs his arm. "No, wait—"

"Let go." His voice is quiet but fierce.

Startled by his tone, she lets go of his arm. Jay turns, opens the classroom door and walks inside. Abby rushes after him, stopping the door with her hand before it closes. She yells into the classroom, "Jay Kepler, you are the worst best friend ever!"

Suddenly, Mr. Smith, the principal, grabs her by the arm and yanks her back into the hallway. *Now what?* Mr. Smith pulls her along, opens the front doors of the school and ushers her outside.

"I don't understand. Am I being *expelled?*" Abby asks.

"I'm sure they'll explain everything," says Mr. Smith. He nods his head in the direction of Abby's parents, who are waiting next to a "RENT-UR-SELF" moving truck. She sees that her red car is parked right behind it.

Growing more and more confused by the minute, Abby

walks up to them. "What's the truck for?" she asks. "Are we moving?"

"Just get in the truck," her father says gruffly. Abby gets in the cab and sits between them. The truck backfires as it pulls out. Abby turns around to see that it's towing her car behind it. They ride along in silence for a moment. Abby, squished between her mother and father, looks from one to the other, waiting for some explanation. "Is somebody going to tell me what's going on?" she finally asks.

Abby's dad throws her mom an exasperated look. She throws him a "please be patient" look right back. "You can't go to high school anymore, Abby," she says, finally.

"Why not?" Abby knows she's been late a few times, but she's never heard of anyone getting kicked out of school for just *that*.

"Because it's time to grow up," says her father, still in that gruff voice.

"Bob," says Abby's mother. Then she turns to Abby and says in a more gentle tone, "Sweetheart, while the house is being fumigated there just really isn't room for you. So your dad and I were talking--"

"We found you an apartment," her dad cuts in.

"A what?!" Abby asks. Now she really knows everyone has gone nutty!

"An apartment," says her mother. "To live in."

"By *myself?*" asks Abby.

They continue driving until they reach an apartment build-ing on the other side of town. When they get out, her parents begin unloading the truck. One by one, they carry in boxes that say "ABBY - CLOTHES" and "ABBY - BOOKS" and "ABBY - KEEPSAKES."

"It's a very safe neighborhood," says her mother.

"Is that what you call it? I call it pricey," grumbles her father.

"Your dad and I paid the security deposit, but the first month's rent is your responsibility," adds her mother, as if he has not spoken. They continue carrying boxes inside; Abby scurries behind them. Soon, boxes are everywhere.

"I'll get the last load," says her father. He goes back out. Her mother hands Abby a page from the newspaper— the Want Ads.

"You're going to need a full time job," says her mother. "I circled some good ones--"

"I can't go to school *and* have a job," Abby interjects.

"Oh, well, if you're ready for college--" She calls out to Abby's father, "Honey, she wants to go to college!"

"No!" Abby cries, alarmed. "Not yet!"

"Never mind," her mother calls out again.

"Mom, I'm just a kid! I can't live here by myself!" says Abby. Her father walks back in carrying the last box.

"Don't be so dramatic. Lots of girls your age have their own apartments," her mother says.

"*I* moved out at *eighteen*," her father announces.

"But I'm not eighteen," Abby points out.

"No, you're twenty-one," her father says.

"Twenty-two today," her mother says brightly. "Happy Birthday, sweetheart."

"What are you talking about?!?" Abby is sure her parents have lost their minds.

"Let's go, Sue," says her father, clearly impatient to be on his way.

"No! Don't go!" cries Abby.

"Just remember, we did this out of love," says her mother, giving her a kiss.

"Yeah, tough love," her father adds under his breath.

"*Bob!*" scolds her mother.

He softens and kisses Abby on the cheek. "You'll be fine, pumpkin," he says and then he leaves. Abby looks at her mother, who gives her one last hug and kiss. "Come see us anytime," she says. "Except Wednesdays. That's our bowling night." Then she too leaves, shutting the door behind her.

Abby stands there alone and stunned, amidst her boxes. She suddenly sees one box that is marked "ABBY - HIGH SCHOOL MEMORIES."

"High school *memories?*" she says. How can that be? She opens the box, flipping past a few photos, including the awful one her dad took that morning in her room. Then she pulls out a framed photograph of herself in a graduation cap and gown, holding up her high school diploma.

Abby is totally confused. And then, all of a sudden, she's not confused any more. No, it's crystal clear. Candle Number 9... Sitting at the kid's table...The saleswoman saying, "Let's get you into something more *age appropriate*" ...Miss Duffy thinking she was the new substitute teacher... Jay backing away from her... Her father saying, "You're twenty-one"... Her mother adding, "Twenty-two today. Happy Birthday." Abby realizes, with horror that she has just wished away what was left of her teen years.

11

～ **"Oh** no. No no, no! This isn't what I wanted!" moans Abby. She rushes to the window. The truck is pulling away from the curb, leaving her red sports car parked in front of the building. Abby turns back to the empty apartment. *"Celeste!"* she cries. She looks around the room, waiting for her Birthday Fairy to appear. "I need to talk to you! Right now!" No Celeste. Frantically, Abby digs through her handbag to find the Wish List, now quite crumpled.

"Wish number three. That's it. That should work," she says to herself. She digs for the magic Candles and the Lucky Duck matches. She lights a match.

"Please work, please work, please," she begs. She lights Candle #3, blows out the match. *When I'm sixteen I'll decorate my room the way I want.* She blows out the candle.

DING-DONG! The doorbell rings. Abby jumps up and runs to look out the peephole in the door. Just as she had hoped, Celeste is standing there, wearing a candy pink wool suit with a bow at the waist. "Decorator's Delight!" she calls out cheerily.

Abby flings open the door. "Celeste! I'm so glad you're here!"

she cries.

Celeste strides past Abby into the room wheeling a decorator's portfolio cart of wallpaper rolls and fabric sample books.

"Me too," says Celeste. She looks around the space. "Okay. Nice. Lots of potential." She takes out a clipboard and starts walking around the apartment, making notes.

"I need your help," Abby begins.

"You sure do. Maybe some wallpaper--"

"No, no wallpaper."

"Paint then. Let's look at some samples," Celeste suggests.

"No, listen to me. Your magic candles made a *mistake.*"

"Candles don't make mistakes, " Celeste says. "People do."

"I made a wish but it wasn't really my wish," Abby says, ready to cry.

"How about some curtains?" offers Celeste.

"No!"

"Ooh, bad decision," says Celeste. "You need privacy. You're alone. You're a woman--"

"No, I'm not! I'm not a woman!" Abby interrupts, practically shouting. "I'm sixteen years old! I made a wish--" she grabs the list. "Wish # 9. I didn't want to BE an adult! I just wanted to be *treated* like one!"

"The Candles have their own logic," Celeste explains. "They

don't always give you what you want. Sometimes they give you what you need. And, sweetie, you need drapes, pronto."

"I don't need drapes!" Abby cries. Celeste, startled, stops. "I need my life back!" Abby continues. "I just wished away my friends, my Sweet Sixteen Party, my Senior prom--" She grabs the framed graduation photo and holds it up. "I missed graduation! I need to take that wish back!"

"Oh, sweetie. I'm afraid that's not possible," says Celeste sadly. "The Candles and your Wishes go together. Since there's no do-over wish on your List, I'm afraid when midnight comes, this--" she gestures to the box-strewn apartment, "is your life."

"But--"

Celeste's cell phone rings and she holds up a finger for quiet. "Decorator's Delight," she chirps into the phone. "Yes. On my way." She clicks off. "Slipcover emergency. Gotta run." She grabs her portfolio and strides out the door.

"Wait!" Abby cries, running out after her; she smacks into her landlord, a burly guy who does not look like he has a warm or fuzzy bone in his extra large body.

"Tryin' ta run out on the rent?" he says with a hint of menace.

"No!" she says. Abby strains to see around him, but unfortunately, Celeste is gone.

"Good," he says, leaning close to her. Hit by a foul blast of his bad breath, Abby reels back. He shoves a threatening rent notice at her. "First month is due in three days," he adds. "Pay up or *get out*."

Abby grabs the notice, turns and runs back into her apartment. She slams the door behind herself, locking the deadbolt. She spies the Wish List on top of her "High School Memories" box. "Stupid wishes! Why did I ever write you down!" she says. But then, ever the optimist, she gets an idea. And it's a good idea too. One of the wishes is written in *pencil*. She takes a big pink eraser and busily scrubs away at Wish #4 ("I'll like Sushi"). After a few minutes, Abby frowns. The words are still there.

Next, she tries hairspray, acne cream, shampoo, dish liquid, deodorant, bleach, various types of cleansers and finally, nail polish. She carefully paints over the words with the pale pink varnish. There! That ought to do it. She sits back, admiring her handiwork. Wish #4 is gone. She did it! But her triumph is short-lived. A magical shimmer hovers over the page, as the words, *I'll like Sushi* come right through the nail polish. Disappointed, she yells at the Wish List, "I hate sushi and I always will!"

She gets up and paces frantically, glaring at the List as she walks by it. Suddenly she stops. Something she sees on the List catches her eye. "Hey..." she says. "What about you, Wish Number Fourteen?" *When I'm sixteen, my parents will finally understand me.* She runs to get Candle #14 and quickly lights it. "This has to work," she says before blowing out the match and the candle.

She dashes out of her apartment, jumps in her car and drives over to her parents' house. When she arrives, she sees that it is still buzzing with wasps that fly in and out of the windows. A silver, Twinkie-shaped camping trailer is parked in the driveway, its striped awning extending out onto the front lawn. The awning is lined with tiki lights. Under it, her parents have created a nifty outdoor living area. There's a big red grill, a table and three chairs on which there's a flyswatter and a half-played game of gin rummy. Nearby there's a TV set in front of a pair of comfy armchairs, a side table that holds a lamp and a framed picture.

Seeing all this, Abby lets out a nervous breath. "Please understand," she whispers. She hurries to the trailer, reaching for the door just as it opens. Her father comes out, wearing the beekeeper's hood and holding a plate with two uncooked hamburgers.

"Abby!" he says.

"Hi, Daddy," Abby replies.

"Honey, look who's here," he calls over his shoulder. Abby's mom emerges from the trailer wearing her own beekeeper's hood and carrying a plate with buns, tomatoes and lettuce.

"Hello, sweetheart," she says.

"Hi, Mom," says Abby. Her mother breezes past her to the grill where her dad is putting the hamburgers on to cook. They take off their hoods.

"Shouldn't you be at your own place, unpacking those boxes?" her mother asks.

"Yeah, but I missed you guys," says Abby, trying to stay calm.

"Aw, that's sweet. But we're kind of busy right now." Abby's mom sits in one of the armchairs and picks up her hand of cards. "Your turn, dear," she says to Abby's dad.

"What's the use?" her father says. "Twenty-two cards in my hand and I still can't play!"

"Can't this wait?" Abby asks.

"Of course. What's up?" her mother says. Without looking, her mother smashes a wasp on the table with her swatter. She seems very practiced at the maneuver. Abby tries hard to maintain her self-control. She can't believe they're being so nonchalant.

She sits down and faces them.

"Well, I have something important to discuss with you and I thought if you really *listen* to me, you might *understand*." She glances over at her father; he's looking at his cards and doesn't seem in the least bit understanding or even interested.

"*Bob,*" chastises her mother.

"What?" he says testily. "I'm *listening.*"

"We're listening," her mom says, looking at Abby now.

"Even if it sounds crazy?"

"I listen to your father all the time," her mother points out.

"What's that supposed to mean?" her father says, defensively.

"Go on, sweetheart," says Abby's mother.

"This morning, when I woke up, I was sixteen years old," begins Abby. She waits for them to laugh, but they nod, listening intently. "I thought this was going to be the best day of my life. Then this Birthday Fairy appeared and gave me these." She puts the Sweet Sixteen Birthday Candles and the Lucky Duck matches on the table. Abby's dad picks up the matches.

"What do you know? Honey, look." He hands Abby's mom the matches.

"Well, that brings back memories, doesn't it?" she says.

"What? What memories?" asks Abby.

"Your father took me to the Lucky Duck Chinese Restaurant on the night you were born."

"I had the orange chicken," her father says.

"We thought it was an omen," says her mother, tearing up. "We always felt so lucky to have a daughter as wonderful as you."

Tears spring into Abby's eyes too. "Really?" she asks.

"Really," says her mother.

"Then you'll understand when I tell you I need to go back to high school and I need to live here, with you. I'm not ready to have a job and my own apartment! Tell me you understand."

Abby's mom looks lovingly at her daughter. "Look behind you, Abby." Abby looks behind her. On the side table next to the chair is the framed photo of eight-year-old Abby wearing the sparkly plastic tiara and eight-year-old Jay, both dressed up in adults' clothing. "Ever since you were a little girl, all you wanted was to be exactly what you are now. Beautiful and independent. I remember the day we took this picture. You wanted a "grown-up" birthday party. All dressed up in my pearls and high heels - you were never happier. But being grown up is different than dreaming about it, isn't it?" her mother says.

"Yes," says Abby. *Is that ever true!*

"We understand you," her mother continues.

Abby gasps back tears. "You do?!" She has been waiting to hear these very words.

"Uh-hm. You're scared your childhood is over and with it all the best times of your life."

"Yes!" Abby says. They really *do* understand!

"You probably wanna just turn back the clock and start over," says her father.

"Yes! Yes! That's exactly what I want to do!" cries Abby.

"Boy, I know that feeling," her father says. Abby throws her arms around him.

"Then I'm still your little girl?"

Her father puts his arms around her. "You'll always be our little girl, pumpkin." Abby clings to him, relieved. He keeps waiting for the embrace to end, and when it doesn't, he mouths "Help me" over her head. Abby's mom understand what he's trying to tell her, jumps up and cries, "Look! Wasps!" Abby looks up for a moment and her father uses the opportunity to peel her off.

"Time to go, pumpkin," he says. "Drive safe."

"And don't forget these." Her mother shoves the candles, matches and framed photo of Abby and Jay into her hands. Her parents practically fall over each other as they race to the door of the trailer. Abby follows them.

"But I thought you understood," she says in a small voice.

"We do. Adulthood is hard," says her father. "Sometimes things get... buggy."

"Bye now, sweetheart!" her mother says. Before Abby can answer, they shut the trailer door in her face. While Abby stands there, stunned, the door opens, and her parents pop their heads out. "Love you!" they trill. Then they slam the door again and lock it.

Abby suddenly flashes back to this morning, when she slammed the door in her parents' faces. So that's what that feels like. She can hear the low mumble of her parents talking and laughing inside the trailer. She looks down sadly at what she's holding: the candles and matches and the picture of herself with Jay. That's all she has right now. Sighing, she tucks every-thing in her designer handbag and heads for her car.

When she walks down the driveway, Abby is mildly surprised to find Logan Buchanan leaning on her car. He's looking right at her, a big smile painted on his handsome face. Abby smiles back.

"Hi, Logan," she says.

"Hey. Cool ride," he replies.

"Yeah, you said that this morning," she reminds him.

"Huh." Brilliant and witty he is not.

"So... what are you doing here?" asks Abby.

"Party." He nods in the direction of the house across the street. Abby follows his gaze and see loads of kids streaming toward Krista's house. The gate to Krista's backyard is arched with yellow balloons. A glittery sign says *"Happy Sweet Sixteen, Krista!"*

"Oh. Right. I wasn't invited," Abby says.

"Huh," repeats Logan.

Abby stands there in the awkward silence. Wow. She never noticed before that Logan's not exactly a clever conversationalist. In fact, as cute as he is, he's kind of boring. Just when she's ready to give up on him, he suddenly looks alive.

"Hey!" he says.

"Yeah?" she says, hopefully.

"Will you do something for me?" he asks.

"Sure," says Abby..

"Take a picture of me with your car." He hands her his cell phone.

"Sure, um--" says Abby, taken aback.

"Thanks. It's what I want when I'm your age." He poses, cheesily, next to the car. Abby takes the shot.

"There ya go," she says, handing him back the phone.

"Cool," he says, looking at the picture. "Oh, man, that's hot. I can't wait to show Krista!" He takes off, still gazing at the image on his phone.

Abby watches him walk toward the party. She has spent so much time dreaming about him. But for the first time, she realizes that everything she believed about him was just that: a dream. Logan is not her dream guy. Sure, he's handsome. But he's not interesting or smart or fun like her best friend Jay. Just then she looks across the street and there is Jay, all dressed up and on his way to the party. He looks good. No, better than good. He looks terrific. Funny she never noticed it before. Abby takes off across the street like a shot, which, in her high heels, is no easy feat.

Abby tackles Jay in a bear hug, knocking him off balance. They fall against a car and she pins him to the hood. Nearby, a gardener in a flowered jacket and big hat is trimming some shrubbery with huge hedge clippers.

"Gotcha!" cries Abby.

"Get off me," Jay says, clearly embarrassed. Some other kids walk by, looking at them and smirking. Jay wriggles out of Abby's embrace. She holds his arm tightly. He tries to get away from her, but she uses her whole body as leverage.

"You have to believe me, Jay," she says. She knows she doesn't have much time so she speaks in a rush. "You're my best friend and it's my sixteenth birthday and I got these magic candles at the bus stop this morning? Remember? This big car pulled up and Joey Lockhart got out and kissed me--"

Jay turns to some of the kids who are watching and says, "I don't know her."

"You were there! You saw him!" Abby pleads. "Jay, you *have* to remember!"

"Let. Go." Jay is desperate to escape her.

"Not until you listen to me. Give me five minutes."

Jay looks around. "Four," he counters.

The gardener looks over at them, and when she pushes her hat back, Abby sees that she is Celeste. Somehow her presence gives Abby the courage to continue.

"Okay. I know this is hard to believe, but we're best friends and I can prove it."

She pulls the half-heart "BFF" pendant on the chain out from where it was tucked under the collar of her dress.

"What about this?" she says.

"So?"

"Look at your key ring," she tells him.

Jay digs in his jeans pocket and pulls out his key ring. The other half of the "BFF" heart pendant dangles next to his house key. He gulps, a little freaked. Abby takes her necklace off over her head and holds out her hand for Jay's key ring. He hands it to her.

Celeste looks over as Abby carefully puts the two halves of the heart together. Celeste winks, and with a magical shimmer, the two halves of the pendant become one. The front says "BFF" and when Abby turns it over, they can both see what is engraved on the back of the pendant. Jay reads the words out loud:

To Abby. Happy Sweet Sixteen. Love, Jay

"You gave this to me *this morning*," Abby says, hopefully. "For my sixteenth birthday."

Jay blinks. It's cloudy, but images are coming into his mind. Jay putting his jacket around Abby's shoulders at the bus stop…

Abby lifting the "BFF" half-heart pendant out of the box...
Abby and Jay talking in the chem lab... Abby and Jay sitting on
the hood of the car at lunchtime... Abby looking at him, laughing and smiling... Abby twirling happily in front of him in the
boutique, wearing the party dress.

"Abby?" says Jay, looking at her with recognition.

"You remember?" she asks. Hope makes her voice quiver a
bit.

"I think so," he says.

"So, you believe me?"

"Yeah," he says. Crazy as it seems, he does. "I do." Abby
throws her arms around him and this time, he doesn't pull away.

Behind them, Celeste is pleased with a job well done on Abby
and Jay and on the shrubbery, which now sports a whimsical
new rabbit topiary. She walks behind it and is gone.

Abby lets Jay go and turns to the other kids on their way to
Krista's party.

"He believes me!" she calls out.

"Whoa. Volume," says Jay. Abby plops down against the
car hood, suddenly realizing she still hasn't solved her biggest
problem. "This doesn't change anything," she says. "And when
midnight comes, I'm stuck like this forever."

He leans on the car next to her. "Lemme see the List." She
digs it out of her purse and she reads along with him, over his

shoulder.

"You've already used one, two, seven, eight and *nine*--" he says pointedly.

"Skip ahead," says Abby, irritated that he always seems to state the obvious.

"I can't believe you wasted a wish on sushi."

"I was eight. I had a very unsophisticated palate," says Abby.

"Had?" Jay inquires dryly.

Abby bumps shoulders with him. He grins. She looks at his face as if for the first time. He's really handsome. How had she not seen it before?

"You're a great best friend, Jay," she says.

"You think?" he says, scanning her face for what he hopes he might see. Could she ever see him as more than a friend? But then he's all business again. "C'mon. Clock's ticking." He looks back down at the list. "Most of these are kind of useless since you're already an adult. That leaves fourteen, fifteen and Logan Buchanan."

"Yeah, about that--" Abby says. How to explain that her fascination with Logan has just shriveled and died? The guy, it has to be said, is a dud.

"Wish Number Fifteen was always my favorite," Jay says. *When I'm sixteen, I'll have the Best Party Ever.* "But you're not sixteen anymore." They sit there a moment, awash in the sadness of Abby having missed that moment. She rests her head on his shoulder. He smiles, a bittersweet smile. He could never tell her that this moment is his favorite moment of the entire day.

"Hey," he says. "I kinda have to make an appearance at Krista's party. Do you, um, want to come with me?" He looks at her and then quickly adds, "Not as my *date* or anything."

"No. Of course not," she quickly agrees.

"Well?" He is waiting.

And at that exact moment, Abby finally sees the truth in Jay's face, in the way his eyes shine when he's close to her. Jay *really* likes her. As more than a best friend. Her heart swells and so does her smile.

"I'd love to go with you, Jay," she says. He offers her his arm and together, they walk toward Krista's house.

Abby and Jay walk into the backyard through the arch of yellow and purple balloons. The party is already happening and it looks like the whole junior class is there. Abby looks around; everything is perfect, just the way she would have wanted it. There's even a live band on a small stage and, to her surprise, her brother Mike is the lead guitar player and singer. From the stage, Mike catches sight of her. "Heyyyyy!" Mike calls out into the microphone. "Give a shout-out to my big sis, Abby, every-body."

"Hey, Abby!" everyone calls out.

"You're super old, Abs, but you're still cool!" Mike jumps into a big lead guitar solo with the band.

Abby turns to Jay. "So, Mike can really play?"

"Yeah. Something just clicked with him this year. He got serious about playing guitar. He's getting paid really well for this gig." But Abby is distracted by someone walking toward them across the lawn.

"Uh-oh," she says, recognizing Krista. Krista sees them and smiles, a big happy smile. She waves enthusiastically, a different Krista than Abby has ever seen before. Jay waves back. Abby looks from one to the other like they're both aliens or something.

"Did I miss something? I mean, besides senior year?" she asks Jay.

Krista gets there before Jay can answer. She's happy and light, a wholly different person. She hugs Jay and turns to Abby as Jay backs away.

"Hi! I'm so glad you could make it!" she says warmly.

"Yeah. I'm... Abby Jensen," Abby says cautiously, realizing Krista may not know her, now that she's an adult.

"I know, silly. We're *neighbors!*" Krista giggles.

"Yes. Neighbors. Your party looks awesome."

"Thanks to your parents," Krista says. "They found all these amazing decorations in their garage after their house was infested by wasps. I guess they were left over from your Sweet Sixteen Party, but never got used for some reason. So they just gave them to me!"

"Lucky you," says Abby dryly.

"I know, right?! Anyway, you're just in time for the big celebration."

Abby turns to see Jay, who is now on stage with Mike.

"Thanks for coming everybody!" says Jay, his voice amplified by the microphone. A cheer goes up from the crowd. "Man.

This is a dream come true for me." The crowd responds with another cheer. Abby is totally confused. What is Jay talking about?

"What's happening?" Abby asks Krista. Beaming, Krista nods back to the stage, where Mike raises Jay's arm over his head.

"Jay Kepler, ladies and gentlemen," says Mike's amplified voice. "Our new... STUDENT. BODY. PRESIDENT!" An even louder cheer goes up from the crowd. Abby's mouth drops open in surprise.

"Thank you," says Jay. "I want to recognize my campaign manager, Krista Cook." Abby whips a look at Krista. She's smiling at Jay, happily. "What all of you don't know is that I really wanted this, but I was too afraid to try. I couldn't have done it without your help, Krista." Jay leads a loud cheer for Krista. She beams and waves.

"Hey, and the vote was UNANIMOUS!" adds Mike. There are more cheers and whistles, as Mike slaps Jay on the back. Jay jumps off the stage. The cheering crowd parts for him as he walks toward Abby. She stands there, incredulous.

"*You're* Student Body President?"

"Yup."

"*I* was Student Body President," says Abby.

"Oh, yeah. Weird," Jay says, remembering.

"I thought with me out of the way, Krista would win," says Abby.

"Krista? She hates competition," Jay says.

"Krista?" Abby is sure there has been some mistake. "Our Krista?"

"Yeah. I think without you in her life, she just didn't have a reason to compete for anything. She's kind, super-helpful, a good listener and a great friend. You two would like each other. If, y'know, you were the same age." Before Abby can digest all this astonishing information and respond, the kids crowd around Jay and hustle him off.

Abby is left looking around. *This was supposed to be my party,* she thinks, sadly. *Mine.* She's seeing it from the outside now; she's no longer part of this world. She spies Logan and Krista. He's showing her the picture Abby took on his cellphone of him leaning on her red sports car. Krista puts her arms around his neck and they nuzzle noses, happily. This makes Abby even sadder. She doesn't even like Logan anymore, but the loss of her dream is a disappointment.

Although she is standing in the midst of a crowd, she feels very, very alone. As Mike and his band kick into another song, she walks out of the Sweet Sixteen party that should have been hers... all by herself. Abby walks to her car as the sun slowly sinks behind the Jensen's still-buzzing house. The tiki lights around the trailer awning suddenly go out. On the other side of the street, party lights glow from Krista's backyard over the rooftop of her house. Abby stands at her car, feeling lost. She's a stranger in both places; she no longer belongs in either.

She gets into the car and sits at the wheel for a moment. Then she straps on her seatbelt, deliberately places her hands on the wheel and drives away. The red sports car moves slowly away from the Jensen house. In fact, it moves more slowly than any of the other cars; drivers honk and veer around her. Abby grips the wheel, rigid and tense. This is the first time she's driven at night and it scares her. Suddenly, the car starts to sputter and slow even more. When it comes to a full stop, she panics. The other cars behind her stop as well, and the drivers angrily blare their horns.

Abby looks at the gas gauge: EMPTY. Oh no! She gets out of the car and dodges traffic to get to the sidewalk. Suddenly, the heel on one of her fabulous grown up pumps snaps off. She removes the shoe, takes a step and— eww. She stops and lifts her bare foot. A grayish wad of gum is strung from the pavement to her sole. She hops to a bus stop bench and, disgusted, peels the gum off of her foot. Just then, a car goes by, splashing her from head to toe with curb water. Could this evening get any worse?

Standing up again, she puts on her ruined shoe and heads

for her new apartment— she can't yet think of it as home— in a jerky, off-balance limp.

Abby lets herself into her apartment. She hobbles over to the box marked.

"High School Memories" and bursts into tears. After a few minutes, she looks around for something on which to wipe her nose. Finding nothing else, she uses her Sweet Sixteen Wish List. That's about all it's good for anymore.

Then the doorbell rings. She gets up and peeks out of the peephole. It's Celeste, wearing a silly Larry's Pizza Hat and uniform.

"Large pepperoni pineapple for Jensen," she chirps.

Abby opens the door, sniffing back her tears. Celeste walks right in with a large pizza box and a bottle of orange juice.

"I didn't order a pizza," she says to Celeste.

Celeste sets the pizza down on one of the unopened moving cartons and removes her hat. "I know. I just thought you could use a friend."

Abby starts to cry - again. Celeste goes over and hugs her. "Oh sweetie. Dry those tears. I'm starving."

"You are?" says Abby.

"Sure. Magical beings have to eat too," explains Celeste. Abby actually smiles a little through her tears.

Some hours later, the pizza is devoured and the juice bottle is empty. A few things have been unpacked: a rug, some throw pillows, a lamp, and the 70s flip-clock from Abby's bedroom at her parents' house. The clock now reads 11:45 p.m. Celeste and Abby are sitting on the one piece of furniture in the room, the old futon from Abby's father's office. The crumpled Wish List sits on the floor next to them.

"This day didn't turn out anything like I thought it would," says Abby thoughtfully. "I can't believe I wasted my Sixteen Wishes on things like beating Krista Cook."

"Yeah. She's really nice now that she doesn't want to destroy you," says Celeste.

"Don't rub it in," Abby says.

"She's a really good friend to Jay," says Celeste, helpfully.

"Better than I was. I didn't even know he wanted to be Student Body President. How could I have been so thoughtless?" Abby asks. "All I could think about was having clothes and parties and popularity. I can't believe those things were so important to me."

"You were sixteen," says Celeste gently.

"But I didn't appreciate it!" Abby says. "Ever since I was little I wanted to grow up. I thought it was the only way to get what I wanted. I guess I didn't appreciate what I already had." Her voice sounds sad.

Celeste picks up the box of Sweet Sixteen Candles and looks inside. "You still have this little number," she says, holding out Candle Number 16.

"Wish Sixteen," Abby says wistfully. "All those years, I saved it for something really special." She thinks of this morning, when she used her gum to stick the photo of Logan to this very spot. Her eyes pool with fresh tears. "Of all the wishes on this list, this is the one I wish I could change."

She begins to pick at Logan's photo... and to her surprise it easily starts to peel away. She pulls a little harder. The gum underneath it stretches until it gives and the photo pops off. She looks at Celeste, shocked.

"Wow, that gum is still really fresh," observes Celeste.

Abby looks at the photo, stunned for a moment, and then at the blank spot next to Wish #16. An idea is forming in her brain, bubbling up and over, just like the blue goo in chem lab. She jumps up and runs to the box that says "High School Memories." She digs through it and takes out the awful photo her father took of her that morning. Then, with trembling hands, she brings it back to the List. She looks at Celeste, her face a mix of hope and fear. "Maybe the rules didn't know about gum," she says.

"There's only one way to find out," says Celeste, encouragingly.

Abby's hands are really shaking now and she has to stop to steady them. When she does, she uses the gum to stick the photo of herself to Wish #16. For the briefest of seconds, the photo seems to glow. Celeste hands her Candle #16 and the

Lucky Duck matches. There's only one match left in the box. Anxiously, Abby glances at the clock. It now reads 11:59 p.m.

Taking a deep, nervous breath, Abby lights the match. She holds it to Candle #16. The candle lights, its flame bright and true. Then she blows out the match... and blows out the candle.

"I wish I could start this whole day over again," she says in an emotion-choked voice. The photograph of Abby again brightens with a magical glow as the clock flips to 12:00 a.m. "I wish it more than anything I have ever wished for in my whole, entire life!"

15

〜 **Abby's** eyes are blinded by a flash of bright, white light, and she puts her hands up to her face to cover them. Then she hears the three voices sing out, "Surprise!" Trembling with hope, Abby glances at herself in her bedroom mirror. Yes! She's in her pink jammies, hair suffering from a major case of bedhead, pore cleansing strip still plastered to the bridge of her nose. Another quick glance down confirms that her bunny slippers— still clean, still fluffy, not muddied at all— are in the center of the room, right where she kicked them off last night.

Her parents and brother approach her; her mom's arms are outstretched under the plate that holds her birthday cake, blazing with sixteen candles.

"Happy Birthday, Abby!" says her mom.

"Look. Your first sixteenth birthday picture," holding the LCD screen of his camera so Abby can see it.

Abby grabs the camera to look at the picture. Bursting with happiness, she laughs and whoops. Yes! It worked! She's back! "This is a GREAT picture, Dad! This is the best picture I've ever seen in my whole life!" She flings her arms around him in a strangling hug. He looks delighted, if a tad confused. "Thank you, thank you, thank you!" she cries.

"You're welcome, pumpkin," says her dad, looking at her strangely. They are all a bit confused by her massive show of enthusiasm.

"Why don't you make a wish, sweetheart?" suggests her mom.

Abby lets go of her dad and looks at her mom, holding the cake, then at her brother Mike with his dumb little toy guitar. She grins. "I wish...for exactly this," she says firmly. "Everything is *perfect*."

She blows out the candles and sighs happily as her parents look on. Suddenly she remembers. Everything is *not* perfect.

"Wasps!" Abby cries. She shoves her parents aside and practically runs Mike over as she rushes out into the hall. Her parents and brother are totally confused, but they follow her.

"I saw one crawling in the AC vent," Mike says casually. "It's hardly a big deal."

"No!" cries Abby pointing frantically to a ladder in the hallway that leads to the attic. "Not one; *thousands* of them, nesting up there for sixteen years!"

"Sweetheart, we know," says her mother.

"You don't know," Abby says, her words tumbling out in one breathless sentence. "You can't possibly know that the house is going to be totally infested and the wasps will take over the cars and you and Dad will have to live in the driveway and then Joey Lockhart will come and kiss me and I'll get candles and wishes and some really gorgeous clothes and everything will look like it's going to be o.k. but then I'll make a really stupid wish that I didn't have to make and I'll have to grow up and live alone and I'll miss my party and this will turn into the worst sixteenth birthday in the history of sixteenth birthdays!" Abby takes a long deep breath and finally pleads, "You have to call an exterminator now!"

Abby is stopped by the slamming of the attic door above her. Instantly, her hands fly to her head to protect herself from the swarm. But instead of a swarm of wasps, there are only feet— female feet in cute, lace-up shoes. Abby watches those feet as they descend down the ladder.

"Okey dokey. All done," says a familiar voice. Abby peeks out from under her arms. It's Celeste, in her Bugs-B-Gone jumpsuit, carrying an exterminator's tank.

"Whoa, that was some wasp nest. You're very lucky I showed up when I did."

"So everything is going to be okay?" asks Abby, hopefully.

"Better than okay," says Celeste as she starts down the stairs. "Everything is going to be *perfect*."

"Wait," calls Abby's dad. "What do I owe ya?"

"Nothing," says Celeste. She turns around. "Consider it a

very special Sweet Sixteen gift for a very special girl. Happy Birthday, Abby."

"Thank you," Abby says. "For *everything.*"

Celeste smiles at Abby and disappears down the stairs. Abby's parents look at each other, utterly confused.

"You know her?" her father asks.

"Oh yeah. That's Celeste," says Abby with a small, private smile.

"Oh," says her mom. Clearly she does not get it.

Abby skips past her parents to her room. Over her shoulder she says, "Mom, maybe you could go on down and start making that special birthday breakfast you have planned for me. I'll be right there."

Her parents look at each other. If they were confused before, they are ten times more confused now. What is going on with Abby today? It's like she's been magically transformed into the world's most polite, accommodating, appreciative and slightly psychic daughter.

Abby hurries into her room and goes straight to the armoire. She opens it.

Her Wish List is stuck to the closet door. She takes it down, kisses it and crumples it up along with the photo of Logan. She tosses both of them into her trash can.

Then she sees something on her desk— her jewelry box. She

opens it and takes out the wad of cash. From somewhere in the house, she can hear Mike start singing an *a cappella* version of the song she heard him play with his band when she was in the grips of the magic. Abby looks at the money as she listens to him sing. She knows exactly what she has to do.

A few minutes later, dressed and ready for school, in her most comfy jeans and favorite red jacket, she skips downstairs. Her birthday breakfast is sitting on the table. She's in a hurry, but she takes a few forkfuls of the scrambled eggs and a slice of the bacon. Yum! Mike is "playing" his toy guitar and still singing the song he's writing. Her parents are seated at the table, drinking coffee and trying not to wince. Abby gently pulls the toy guitar out of his hands.

"What the--" he begins.

But Abby silences him by handing him the wad of cash. "This is for you," she says. "I was saving it for my Sweet Sixteen party, but I think you need it more."

"For what?" Mike asks, stunned.

"A real guitar," says Abby with a little shrug. "I think you're really talented."

Mike takes the wad of cash and wraps his arms around Abby, crushing her in a great big, brotherly bearhug.

"Thank you, Abs," says Mike.

"I love you, Mike," Abby replies. Abby's parents sit there with their mouths wide open; they are so surprised that they just about fall out of their chairs. Abby grabs a muffin and one more piece of bacon off the plate of food and hurries out the door. "Thanks for the yummy breakfast, Mom," she calls out. "Love you!"

"Love you too," her parents call back. They don't know what's come over her, but boy, oh boy, do they ever like it!

Abby comes down the driveway just in time to see Krista walking from her house to her brand new yellow car carrying a box full of "Vote 4 Krista" posters.

Without a second's hesitation, Abby runs across the street toward her. "Krista!" she yells. Krista looks alarmed. She hurries to her car as if Abby is about to tackle her. Abby rushes up and blocks the driver's side door.

"We need to talk," Abby says.

"I have nothing to say to you," says Krista coldly.

"I just have one quick question," Abby says.

"No, you cannot have a ride," retorts Krista.

"I don't want a ride. I want to understand. What did I ever do to you?" asks Abby.

"Go. Away." Krista says.

"Not until you answer me. Why don't you like me?"

"You really don't know, do you?" Krista says, realizing suddenly that Abby is being honest.

"Not a clue," Abby says.

Krista looks away. She is not sure if she wants to go there with Abby. But she finally decides if Abby can be honest, so can she. "It was during third grade," she begins. "Jay and I were best friends. Then you moved to town."

"It was my birthday," says Abby, remembering now. "Jay and I made a pact...We were going to be best friends forever." She remembers something else too: the photo that she kept of herself with Jay didn't tell the whole story. Krista had been there too, all primped and pretty. She'd been holding Jay's other hand for the photo, but they were separated away when Abby pulled him closer. Krista had looked hurt but Abby, being eight and not too sensitive, hadn't really noticed much. Or if she had noticed, she hadn't cared. Jay was her friend now. Krista would just have to deal with it. But now, all these years later, Abby understands what she did and how it must have wounded Krista. It wasn't all Krista's fault. She had played in their feud all these years.

"I stole your best friend," Abby says quietly,.

"On my birthday," Krista adds.

"After that, Jay and I did everything together. That must have been so horrible for you," says Abby.

"It was," Krista says. "I felt like a loser."

"Krista," Abby says. "If I could turn back the clock and change that day, I would. I am so sorry."

"You are?" Krista is not sure whether to believe her.

"Any chance you can forgive me?" asks Abby.

"I don't know," Krista says, reluctantly. "I made my own vow that day."

"Which was…" Abby says.

"I vowed to win at *everything* so you'd never get anything you wanted ever again," Krista says.

"Wow," says Abby. "You did a great job."

"Thank you," Krista says and then is silent. The one-time enemies stand there, letting the moment sink in. All the energy seems to have gone out of their feud.

"Hey," says Abby, getting excited. "Imagine if you used your powers for good instead of evil."

"Like what?" Krista asks.

Abby takes a "Vote 4 Krista" poster and holds it up. "Do you really want to be Student Body President?" she asks.

"Honestly?" says Krista. "No. It's exhausting having to win all the time."

"Well, if you want to drop out, I know somebody who would *love* to take your place," says Abby with a grin.

Krista, who is beginning to understand, grins back.

When Krista's yellow car pulls into the parking lot, Logan and Ted stand back, swooning. Krista gets out of the car.

"Hey, Krista--" Logan says. Then he sees Abby get out of the passenger seat, a rolled up poster in her hand.

"And Abby--" says Ted, clearly puzzled.

"Cool ride," says Logan.

"Thanks," Abby and Krista say in unison and stride right past them. Grinning, they walk side-by-side through the crowd and up to the big yellow school bus idling at the curb just as Jay gets off the bus. He's holding the gift he brought to the bus stop for Abby -- except this time, there was no Abby. She never showed. Then he sees her.

"You're a terrible best friend," he says.

"No, I'm not," Abby says, sure of herself.

"Yes, you are. I had to take the bus. By myself. Where were you?" he asks.

"I got a ride," Abby says, stepping aside to reveal Krista standing behind her.

"You two! In one vehicle. And it didn't, like, explode?" Clearly, Jay is stunned.

The girls look at each other and grin.

"Nope," Krista says.

"We have a surprise for you," Abby adds.

"Why?" says Jay. "It's not my birthday."

"No, it's mine," Abby says.

"And mine," adds Krista.

"And all we want is for *your* dream to come true," Abby says.

"What dream?" Jay says. He looks a little worried.

Abby unfurls the poster. The name "Krista" is crossed out with a big fat black marker. The poster now says, "Vote 4 Jay!"

"You're now the only person running for Student Body President," says Krista.

"So you'll win for sure," Abby adds, happily.

A smile begins to break out on Jay's face. "Think so?" he asks.

"Absolutely!" Abby says as she watches his small smile turn into a major grin. So Jay really did want to be student body president! Abby is sorry that it took her so long to understand this. But she's glad that she finally did, and that she's able to help her friend get the thing he wants so badly. What else has she been missing about Jay all these years? She's hopes she's not too late to find out.

Abby's words come true. Jay wins the election and is named Student Body President. Later that night, he stands on the little stage at Krista's house and faces all the kids who are gathered for their joint Sweet Sixteen celebration. Mike stands next to him and behind them are the members of the band with a different lead singer, waiting to start playing.

"Jay Kepler, ladies and gentlemen," says Mike. "Our new... STUDENT. BODY. PRESIDENT!" Mike raises Jay's hand over his head, while Abby and Krista lead the crowd in a cheer.

Jay looks out at the lawn, the lights, and the decorations. He realizes that this party represents the best of both Abby and Krista and the whole thing glows like a jewel in the night. Jay takes the microphone. "Thanks, everybody. And a special thanks to our two birthday girls. Happy Sweet Sixteen, Abby and Krista! I couldn't have done it without you. *Both* of you."

Abby and Krista link arms and wave to the crowd as the band kicks into a song. Mike hangs around onstage with them, wanting so badly to belong. Down in the audience, Krista leans close to Abby and nods toward the gate. "Look who's here," she whispers. They turn to see Logan coming into the backyard. Abby nudges Krista.

"I happen to know Logan really likes you," says Abby. "Do you like him too? Or was that just an act you put on to make me suffer?"

"I really do like him. Making you suffer was just a bonus." Krista says, honestly.

"Then go talk to him," Abby says.

"About what?" says Krista.

"Ask him about the red sports car he wants to drive some-day," says Abby.

"Sports car?" Krista asks.

"Trust me," Abby says, giving her a gentle shove. "Just do it!"

"Okay," Krista says, grinning as she scampers off to join Logan. *They look good together*, thinks Abby as she watches them. They really do.

Abby looks over at Jay, shaking hands with people in the crowd in front of the stage. Jay catches Abby's eye and smiles. She smiles back at him. The crowd parts for him and he walks toward her. Her smile gets bigger as he gets closer to her, and his smile grows bigger too. Finally, they are face to face.

"Happy Birthday, Abby," Jay says softly.

"Yes it is," she says. "It is now, officially, the best sixteenth birthday in the history of sixteenth birthdays."

"Good. Great in fact," says Jay nodding. "So... I guess you're going to start a new wish list."

"No!" Abby says. "No more wish lists for me. I've got every-thing I could ever want right here."

"Really?" Jay asks, scanning her face for what he hopes to find there.

"Really," Abby says, confirming with the happy look on her face that she actually does like him as more than just a friend.

Up on the stage, the band invites Mike to sing along with their final song. He really sounds good. As they listen, Jay shyly takes Abby's hand, which he's been aching to do all day. She gives his hand an answering squeeze.

As Jay and Abby gaze into each other's eyes, Celeste, in a caterer's apron, walks by with a large silver tray of appetizers. She sneaks a quick glance at the happy couple then smiles, a very contented kind of smile, before vanishing into the crowd. No one notices the little sparkles that hover brightly in the air for just the shortest of seconds after she disappears.

Abby looks at Jay, who is staring at her with such a tender, adoring expression on his face. And then she doesn't see anything else, because she closes her eyes as he leans over to give her the softest, sweetest, birthday kiss in the history of birthday kisses. Ever.